LOVE'S REQUIRED

AJA

SHE LOVES WORDS PUBLISHING

NEWSLETTER SIGN UP

Sign up for my mailing list here:
https://www.
subscribepage.com/passionatefictionbyaja

This is a work of fiction. Any references or similarities to actual events, real people, living or dead, or to real locales are intended to give the novel a sense of reality. Any similarity in other names, characters, places, and incidents is entirely coincidental.

No part of this book may be reproduced in any form or by any means without prior consent of the publisher/author, except brief quotes used in reviews.

Cover design by Young Creations.

DEDICATION

It was my grandmother, Carrie L. Wynn, who taught me that love and time took care of most problems. Her own love, which I witnessed her share with everyone around her, taught me that love was a requirement when dealing with people, especially those hurting or even those hurting you. Either you love them through their hurt or love yourself by moving away from their infliction and then begin to heal. But LOVE is required. So even though she is now in heaven and unable to read this story here on earth, her spirit lives on in any story I write about love.

I thought I would cry while writing this dedication because she meant the world to me but instead, I hear her whisper, "Well done, baby. You now understand."

ACKNOWLEDGMENTS

Special thanks to those that love me through all my imperfections and have shown me that there is no honor in suffering whenever I've felt I had to bear the burden of it.

To my husband, to my children, to my mother, to my writing partner, to my editors, to my graphic designer, to my family and to my closest friends that see the Phoenix in me that can be found in Camille. To Matysha, who never stopped hoping and never stopped asking for Logan. I say to you all, thanks for giving me love, for love is required for us all.

PRELUDE

She'd waited for him to show and though she waited longer than she wanted to, she knew that when he finally touched her, it would erase the sour taste she'd had in her mouth all night. The taste left by loneliness and want.

But he knew she'd wait as long as it took, no matter the hour and no matter what responsibilities she had the next day like teaching her children because she was addicted to him and this addiction wasn't like one had to chocolate—where it was mostly harmless and knowing there was research to support the health benefits to it, one could continue to gorge themselves on it with no guilt. No, this addiction was like crack. Destructive, hard to shake and eventually you'd die from it.

And then he showed up, using the key she'd given him over a year ago so that no one would see him waiting in the hallway at night. He came in to find her standing in the darkened living room with a light from her bedroom casting enough of a glow for him to make out her naked form. He licked his lips, once again pleased that she understood what he needed from her. He only needed a place to feel good for a few hours. A place to forget responsibility for a few hours. He just needed her pleasure and he would have it.

He reached her and pressed his lips to hers and her warm body melted against his and his dick hardened against her tight stomach. She reached for it, stroked it in the palm of her small hand earning a growl from him.

Tired of waiting to have her, because he had to wait all day through meetings and then through dinner at home, he pulled her towards her bedroom and with the light of the lamp, he used it to undress for her, then met her on the bed where he used his lips and tongue on her already wet sweetness. He pulled her into his mouth and made her scream out before slicing the stillness that followed with a hard thrust that she captured inside of her. His pumping was met with her hips rocking beneath him and his groans were met with her loud cries. They were great as lovers, and he intended to keep her as his forever if he could manage.

They reached the end together, her body shaking and his jerking against her, before he pulled her beside him to have her lay her head on his damp chest. They remained like that, content and seemingly happy until the ugly reminder came. This time much earlier and completely out of his control which was becoming the norm lately.

He pulled away from her soft warmth, and out of the bed and went to his pants pocket and grabbed the vibrating phone.

"Hello," he answered.

After a few moments of listening he said, "I'm almost through here. I have what I need for my appointment with my client tomorrow."

More listening before he said, "Okay, Althea. I'll be home in a few." Then he hung up.

He didn't look at her. He couldn't at first. This is the situation that bothered her the most. That he could be called away in the middle of whatever they were doing because he had to be a husband to his wife and even though she knew those were the consequences of their relationship, it didn't make it any easier. Just a moment ago she was clawing at his back as he deep stroked her loneliness out of her and now he was leaving to go back to his wife.

Stupid silly her.

CHAPTER ONE

IT'S OVER...

His words kept taunting her like a broken or skipping record. She wasn't sure which one but knew that they were, in fact, broken. Broken. Torn apart. No longer whole or put together. This is how she felt without his hands brushing against her warm skin – well, it used to be warm. Warm from the light inside of her. From the spirit she allowed to roam free and drift. It's how she encountered him. Without inhibition, without boundaries when she should have had plenty. He was the father of one of her precocious kindergarten students. He was married. He should have been off-limits.

Ali Taylor had a habit of buzzing around the classroom helping to distract her classmates with stories of whimsical tidings. They were so caught up in her depictions of Ali's extraordinary life, they weren't paying attention to Ms. Douglas' story of the *Lion and the Mouse.*

Cami loved Ali's spirit. She loved it so much that she didn't want to hamper it the way most of her teachers tried to hamper *her* when she was that age. Instead, she decided to tell the handsome broad-shouldered man that would sometimes linger outside of the school. He spent time talking to Ali about her day before they'd walk off to the parking lot, and she decided he needed to know all about his enthusiastic daughter. Maybe he could find a way for Ali to share that spirit without creating a distraction for the other students. It seemed he took the most time with the child during those moments. Ali's mother was swifter with her pickup routine and Cami under-stood why, since most parents that tried to do the pickup instead of relying on busing, were in a rush to either return to work or some other errand they needed to complete before the rush.

But Mr. Taylor took his time, which endeared him to Cami. One day when she was on her way out to go to the post office to pick up her latest order of jewelry she would be delivering to her clients that week, she saw him lingering; a great mighty tower among the munchkins being ushered to cars and buses. As she got closer, she found that he was listening as Ali weaved a story of how she escaped the terror of Donovan Williams' hacking cough by flying in the air. Cami stopped so she could hear the story. After a while, Mr. Taylor turned to find Cami enraptured in the colorful tale and instead of asking her what she wanted, he flashed his bright white smile and asked her if she enjoyed Ali's anecdote.

"I did, but I always do. Your daughter has a gift, Mr. Taylor." His lazy smile served as his response before he stroked his daughter's fuzzy braided hair. When he looked back up, his focus was intently on her and he wanted her to know it was. She was sure of this.

"Call me Jay. Mr. Taylor is my father and he's nowhere around, now is he?"

She realized immediately that he was flirting and that should have hastened her to sharing the informal progress report on his daughter and then moving on, but it didn't. She was enjoying the tease. It had been awhile since she had someone to play with.

"Well, Jay, I just wanted to arrange some time to go over how well your daughter is doing. She is such a bright little girl with a bright future in storytelling."

Reading in between the lines, the ones she was

being clear on and the one she shouldn't have even shared.

"I see. Now wouldn't be a good time to go over it since I need to get Ali home, but how about I call you to discuss her progress? While you're not in the classroom, of course."

She hesitated for just a moment. Just long enough to tell herself to move forward and fly free because regardless of the repercussions, life was in the living and she had a feeling this would be a spectacular experience. She scrawled her number down on a piece of tablet paper from her tote bag and passed it to him before squatting down to the keen observer.

"I'd like you to try something for me, Ali."

"What's that, Ms. Douglas?" She asked between her snaggletooth smile.

"Start writing your stories down and ask your mommy or daddy for help. Can you do that for me?"

"But I don't know a lot of words, Ms. Douglas," she whined.

"Don't you worry about that, little one. Use the words you know, okay?" Cami gave Ali her best encouraging smile and the little girl's face lit up before giving Cami a tight hug. She knew there were boundaries that should have existed between teacher and student, but Ali reminded her of another little girl she once knew. A little girl just as uninhibited and free and precocious and excited about the world.

When she stood back up, Mr. Taylor was watching her with curiosity and a hint of longing. "You love my daughter, don't you?" He asked.

Her face warmed with embarrassment before she admitted, "I love all of my children. They make this world interesting."

"That they do, but movies and art are interesting. What I sense in you is a *passion* for what you do." He emphasized the word passion in a way that made her conjure the image of twisted sheets and drawn out moans before she tried to steer her mind back on her passion for the children.

"I do love what I do and these children need someone to be as excited about them making it in this world. They need people who care for them. Don't you agree?"

"Absolutely. If you had been my kindergarten teacher, maybe I would have learned a lot more."

She couldn't speak to how much he knew or whether she could have taught him more. She did know that too much was happening in front of prying eyes, so she remained silent.

"Oh, don't get shy on me now, Ms. Douglas. My

daughter said you have the best laugh in the world. She mimics you just about every day I pick her up from school. Let me hear it some time."

He left her there to watch as he took Ali to his black *Mercedes-Benz CLS400C4*. As he pulled off, Cami wondered what she had started but was sure whatever it was would be fun and intense. But she didn't realize how intense nor did she understand that not all intensity was welcomed. So intense, she turned into one of the women she would laugh at. The one willing to stalk him, hang out at his parked car so she'd be the first person he'd see when he came out of his job. The one calling his cell phone more than a couple times a day hoping he'd answer. She had turned into a monster. A monster in love.

How was it that a man can initially make you feel like you are the most important person in his world after his daughter, but not really being the truth? How was it that over time, he kept chipping away at all the things you held dear, but you stay anyway because you think it will go back to the way it was?

How was it that you were willing to be second or third to everything else just because of a few moments that made you feel suspended in love and in his attention? How was it that you could sell your soul for a lie?

She wondered the answers to her most burning questions but knew she would never get a real answer, not the one that would make her feel any better about her choices. She knew the answer would hurt because it meant she hadn't loved herself enough, that she was willing to accept whatever he gave her. That was why.

If you see me, go the other way.

Jay took her on his business trips when she was on school breaks. He drove them out to Westmoreland County to go on dates where they could be out and not hide in some seedy hotel. They actually had a relationship. Cami was his mistress. Cami had started to become the biggest open secret. You see, there were a few people that already knew Jay was with her. Mrs. Taylor was the only one, it seemed, that didn't know of her husband's mistress of almost two years.

Althea found out about the affair due to an old associate of hers who ran into her at a board meeting. Seeing Althea's wedding band, she incorrectly assumed she had gotten remarried because Jay seemed like he was not married to her.

"No, why would you ask that? Jay and I are still happily married," she said.

The woman looked uncomfortable realizing what she walked into and, believe it or not, wasn't trying to reveal some big secret but being put on the spot, she mentioned seeing Jay with another woman, a young woman, at the movies. Mrs. Taylor tried to make light of it saying, "Jay can sometimes be flirtatious." The other woman said, "No, they were holding hands and even kissed before going into the theater to see the same movie that me and my husband were seeing." She admitted to not knowing what happened after that since she was focused on her own date.

Mrs. Taylor was livid and lit into her husband that night; a night he came in late from being with Cami.

"Who is she, Jay?"

"I don't know what you're talking about, Thea."

"Don't *Thea* me. I know all about the bitch you took to the theater to see the new *Marvel* movie. I thought you didn't want to see it? I guess that's because you had went to see it already, huh?"

He couldn't say anything and wouldn't say anything. Until he figured out what she knew, he was going to play it by ear.

"I bumped into someone if that's what you mean. I did see someone when I went to see the movie."

She looked like she was thinking about it and for a moment he thought that would be enough until her expression said, not a chance.

"So what was the kissing and hugging, huh? Stop lying, Jay."

"I have no idea what someone *thought* they saw but I went to the movies and ran into someone I know. That's all."

"That's all?"

"Yeah."

"Okay, so why didn't you mention you saw the movie, Jay?"

"Because, Thea, sometimes I want to do stuff on my own without having to explain myself each moment. I didn't want to see it with you, okay?"

She looked hurt and he was hoping that emotion would become a distraction, but Althea had been distracted by Jay's words for more than ten years. Ten years of nothing but excuses and lies. She knew they were lies because they were way too smooth. He always had a story for why he didn't answer the phone when she called, why he didn't get in when he was expected, why he wasn't touching her the same way, why he didn't seem to be in to her anymore.

Excuses.

That's all they were.

And she had grown very tired of pretending she didn't know about the women he creeped around with, but this bitch was different. He was seen out with her and that ruined more than her heart. It ruined her reputation of having a loving husband and family at home. And Althea was all about appearances. Between her being active in church ministries and throughout the city, she was seen as the woman that had a giving heart with a loving and loyal family behind her. She often asked Jay to participate in these functions, though he had no interest in them, but in order to make things easier at home he did them. This would usually be the day he had to break his commitment to be somewhere with Cami and that had started to become a stressor on their affair.

If he were available, he would have wanted to spend his time with Cami. He had a better time with her. Between her freakiness in bed, and if he were honest, the way she made him feel like a man, he loved being with her more than he loved being with his wife. But he was not available and if Althea asked him for something, he needed to be present because she would only make his life hell if he didn't. He'd seen it too many times before. There were a couple of times he didn't take her call, or he didn't show up at home on time and there was nothing but ice to deal with when he got in. But being with Camille sometimes made him forget about home. Forget about Althea. Not about Ali. He loved his little girl but honestly, when he was with Camille, he was with Camille.

But things blew up. Everything came out. He did enough damage control that Althea wasn't threatening to leave though he doubted she really wanted to leave anyway. Althea was afraid of having a failed marriage, which is why no matter what he did or didn't do, she'd get over it. All he had to do was be attentive for a while and she was back to feeling like her marriage was on solid ground.

He could never understand that, but it served its purpose for him. He got to have what he needed without the headache of divorce or separation.

But from Cami's point of view, how was she supposed to go the other way when for the past year, the only way to go seemed to be with him, she wanted to know. When she asked him how was she to move on when he had been so persistent in capturing her, he had no response other than giving her the hardness in his dark brown eyes. They were cold and distant when they had once been warm and focused entirely on her.

"She knows now and that has created trouble for me. And I don't like trouble, Cami," he said as he pulled out of her cold arms.

"I didn't tell her though. You know I would never tell her about what we have."

"Had, Cami. Past tense. And it doesn't matter. The moment she found out, we had to be a wrap. What made you think you could call me when I distinctly told you to wait for my call?" He yelled.

"I called because I'd been called into a meeting and walked out without my job. She called the school board, Jay! I needed to talk to you. Don't you understand what this means for me? I don't have a job!"

"I keep telling you this and you don't seem to understand. This. Is. Not. About. You." He clapped his hands to punctuate each word.

She stared at him, her face a manifestation of the torture, the hopelessness, the humiliation, she'd felt over the past few days as he avoided her texts, her calls, any attempt she made to get in touch with him. It was as if he, they, hadn't existed. But she knew they had. The abortion she had two months ago was proof that *they* had existed quite well.

"Don't cry anymore, Cami. It won't help. It has to be over and this is the last time you'll see me. Understand?" He looked her dead in the eye to make sure she understood clearly. His voice didn't waver. He didn't seem conflicted, the way she had imagined he had to have been when he didn't take her calls over the last few days. He seemed sure. "What we had is done. It's over. I don't want you to call me again. Don't text me. If you see me, go the other way."

In fact, he seemed like he never did love her.

Cami sat at her light pink antique desk, which was given to her by her maternal grandmother. It was a passing down gift meant to remind her of her mother's spirit and fondness of the color pink when she was young. She loved this worn piece of furniture that she used as a vanity in her Bohemian decorated bedroom with other odd and mix and matched pieces that came together in a way that only she could make it.

Cami loved this desk as if she'd been gifted with her mother's diamond ring, which had never been recovered from the robbery that claimed her life nearly twenty years ago.

As she chased down the half bottle of Oxycodone pills from her dad's foot surgery from a month ago with a bottle of *Ketel One Vodka*, she looked at herself in the burnished gold oval mirror and forced herself to stare at the monster waiting there. This monster was once golden but now had pale skin and bones with pink swollen eyes surrounded by dark circles from restless nights of worry and fear. No, of course he wouldn't want her. No one would. No one would want her ever again.

She was used up and no longer worth the life that had been given to her to cherish. She had ruined her career, ruined her prospect of ever having a future with him; something he never promised but she had hoped for. She had ruined herself.

What did she have anymore?

She picked up her phone and dialed familiar numbers hoping to say her goodbye before she faded.

And fade, she did.

It's over ...

CHAPTER TWO

"WHOSE CALL ARE you avoiding this time?" Shayna asked Logan as he slid his phone back into the pocket of his crisp light blue uniform top.

"Not a woman, Montane," he lied.

It was in fact a woman he was avoiding but not his usual captured prey that didn't realize they were dead – over – played out. It was his mom. His worrying mother whom he didn't feel like talking to right now.

"Mkay, Graham. Tell me anything. What's the name of the honey you had to run out the station a month ago? What's her name?" Her toothy grin let him know she knew exactly what the corporate bombshell's name was.

"Denise. Her name is Denise and I think she got the drift."

"How can you be so sure?"

"I pressed charges on her ass when she tried to break into my place."

"She did what?"

"Like I said, she tried to break in. She claimed she wanted to get some, and she saw me drag my ass home after my shift, which tells me she was stalking me, mind you. But anyway, she said she wanted to surprise me with some head game."

"Get out of here!"

"Yep."

"And you, Logan Graham, said no." She leveled him with a look of disbelief.

"I said hell no, Montane. Crazy head is not the head I want. Uh-uh. So I called the popo on the hoe." They both laughed and then got silent for a while. Shayna took a sip of her cherry lime drink from *Sonic* and turned to Logan.

"I'm proud of you, Angel," she said using the nickname everyone had taken to calling him at the unit, or house as they called it. He picked it up when all of his responses would make it to the hospital alive. Some of them died after arrival, but he would get them there. That was until some months ago. So now, he hated being called Angel. He never expressed it to anyone, even Shayna, his partner that he spent hours at a time with.

"Proud of what? Putting her in the clank?"

"No, big head. For your promotion. You're at the top now, Graham. The possibilities are endless."

He looked at Shayna and marveled at all that beauty in one person. She was fine. Big hazel eyes, soft kissable lips, luscious body, and a narrow waist. He would have been game to bring her home to celebrate when he moved up from EMT to paramedic, but he'd known since they became partners that she was as interested in Denise as he was. Montane liked women and for him, that was a damn shame.

"Yeah, well. I want to be able to do all I can."

Shayna didn't understand his passion behind those words. Logan had felt helpless when trying to save the life of someone he should or could have been able to save. All she had to do was make a difference choice; leave. Instead, she stayed and died in front of him and there wasn't a damn thing he could do to help her with or without the extra fifteen hundred hours of training to become a paramedic. Either way, he was highly trained and could help more people when he took the call.

His phone buzzed again and when he removed it

from his pocket, he wasn't surprised to see it was his mom calling again. She wouldn't let up until she got to the bottom of what was going on with him. What she didn't understand was that no one could understand this. And since there was nothing to be done, she didn't need to get to the bottom of it. But he couldn't put her off forever and Montane would eventually inquire about all of the ignored calls. That would mean he'd have to avoid another woman and this one would be in close confines with him.

"Hey, Ma."

"Oh, I'm so glad you were free, Logan. I've been trying to reach you for the last couple of days."

"I know. I haven't been avoiding you," he lied. "I've just been really busy. These shifts they have me on since my promotion have been erratic."

Now that was true. Since his promotion, he'd been placed on rotating shifts to get a feel for where his resources would best be utilized. He also had the feeling they would pair him with another partner since Shayna had some limitation in scheduling due to her taking care of her ill mother. Something she rarely spoke of to those that she worked with. Mainly because they spent so much time helping vulnerable, sick, and injured people. Why add to their troubles?

"I understand. I didn't call to make you feel bad,

baby. Do you think you can come to dinner on Sunday?" She asked him, changing the topic to something she'd been trying to get him to do. It had been a month of Sundays, as she put it, since he'd been home to be with the whole family. Logan didn't see it that way. He stopped over once a week; he just had no intention of staying long enough to be pinned into some discussion where they'd want to talk about events that he was working on forgetting.

"I work Sunday, but I'm scheduled to get off at seven. If I'm not dead on my feet, I'll stop by, Ma."

She was getting ready to say something else when the chirp of the radio caught he and Shayna's attention. He turned it up and listened to the operator give details of an unresponsive female found in the Highland Park section of the city on Byran Street. They were about three minutes out and took the call. When he hung up with his mom and pushed the gas to try to help save another life, he wondered how long he could avoid the talk where he told his mom to stop meddling.

Let sleeping dogs die already.

When they arrived at the apartment building, they climbed the stairs and headed to the door at the end of the hall, being sure to check for their safety because as often was the case, the situations were never just about needing medical attention. There were scenarios first responders could find themselves in that endangered their lives.

Seeing no threat, they moved toward the apartment. The wood-framed door was ajar, and they entered an eclectically decorated living room. All sorts of colors swirled into a beautiful display of art. That was the only way he could describe it when he called out, "Life rescue!"

"Back here," a female's voice called out. He and Montane headed back to a woman's bedroom. He approached the kneeling woman holding and crying over a limp light brown body, scarcely covered by a nightgown.

"Ma'am." His rough voice caught the attention of Amara Harper holding Cami's listless body.

"Amara?"

Logan was confused. If Amara is here, who is she holding? It took a moment to register that she was holding beautiful Camille. Camille he could have fallen in love with when he met her in Barbados last year at Noah's wedding. Camille who he would have loved to pull into the closest closet or hotel room to please himself and her, but he knew that she worth more than what he could offer to give her.

Using her as a receptacle was not the treatment this woman deserved.

He needed to triage the situation and as much as he wanted to comfort Amara, he knew that in order to help save her best friend's life, he needed to focus on Camille.

"Okay, doll, I have to ask you some questions." When Amara nodded he continued as he assessed Camille's airway, her respiratory and cardiac functions.

"How long has she been like this?" It was clear she was unconscious and in some sort of induced state.

"I'm not sure but she called me about an hour ago. She sounded horrible, her speech was slurred." She cried.

"What did she take?"

"I think she was drinking and took these." She showed him the bottle of Oxycodone and he passed it to Montane who had already inserted a line for any drugs to be administered. Luckily, she had because she immediately went into her bag to find the reversal medicine for opioid drugs. She immediately infused the line with the fluid and they waited to see if it would have any effect. Camille began to stir.

"Pupils are reactive, blood pressure is stabilizing, skin is still clammy, cool to the touch."

"We've got to move," Logan said, giving Amara instructions on where they were taking her friend.

"Call Noah, Amara. Have him meet you so you're not alone."

CHAPTER THREE

AMARA FARRINGTON PACED BACK and forth in the waiting area of the emergency department of Shadyside Hospital, hoping that someone, anyone, would come out to tell her how her best friend, Cami was doing. She arrived at the hospital driving on the heels of the ambulance that carried her friend who seemed to have been hanging on to her life by a thread. As she rushed to her car to follow Logan and Shayna to the hospital, she called Noah.

Noah, who had been waiting to hear what was going on, was anxious to hear from his wife. As soon as his wife rushed out the house to Cami, she was barely able to tell him why she sprang into action,

"She needs me, Noah. That's all I know," is what

Amara had said when she left out to see about Cami's call. So he waited to hear what had his wife so upset. As soon as he heard her voice on the phone a half an hour later, he knew it was bad and as she tried to push the words through her hiccupped cry, he was already putting his shoes on and grabbing his keys to make it to the hospital to meet her. And now she waited for the doctors to give her some news that would calm her down.

Logan Graham and Noah Farrington sat side-by-side discussing the events.

"I couldn't believe what I was seeing, man. I mean, I couldn't believe she was out like that."

Logan had been trying to wrap his brain around it all from the moment he realized that this wasn't a normal call he responded to. Cami was full-spirited, vivacious, always smiling and if not smiling, intense.

Beautiful.

And yes, a little screwed up.

Something he could tell just by looking at her.

He officially met her for the first time during the rehearsals for his boy's wedding. He was struck by how beautiful she was but then he thought she was just as intense as Amara. But after the wedding when they took the photos, she was the silly one. Making jokes and not doing what the photographer asked at all. He loved it. So naturally, he'd hope that they could share a few playful moments before they headed back to the winter dreariness in Pittsburgh, but as they talked at the bar it became clear she was preoccupied. She was constantly checking her phone, frowning whenever she saw or didn't see something she liked. So he moved on and found a willing tourist to spend some time with.

"I don't know everything, but I know things have been rough for her lately. Sometimes my wife goes into another room to talk to her. I hear her soothing voice murmuring, like she's trying to help Cami through something monumental. But Amara is private, and I respect how protective she is about her closest friend, so I only ask is Cami cool? And she'll say, 'she will be when she learns.'"

"Learns what?"

"Hell if I know. We are talking about women, Lo. What man you know that can figure them out?"

They both sat back in their seats at the same time contemplating the point. Logan was the first to speak up.

"I think with lots of listening and maybe with the understanding that it won't make sense, we can make sense of it." He looked over at Noah who just stared back at him with a blank expression. Then they busted out laughing earning a scowl from Amara who was still pacing in her jeans and one of Noah's white V-neck undershirts she liked to confiscate from his underwear drawer every chance she could get.

"I think you need to go and comfort Doll. You know how she can get when we huddle together for too long."

"That's only because you used to call her Misery."

"And how does she know that, huh?"

"It's called pillow talk."

"Yeah well, you don't sell out your homies when you trying to get laid while lying on your pillow."

"See if you're saying that when it's your woman looking at you all smoky-eyed and wet from hours of loving and asking you for your secrets," Noah said with a grin that brought out the dip in his cheek.

"Too much info, man," Logan said, shaking his head.

"You went there."

"And you're a punk."

Noah didn't deny it, he just looked at his beautiful wife as she took a call on her cell phone. Probably the call she'd been waiting for since she had tried reaching Mr. Douglas, Cami's father. With it being so late, or early, depending on how you saw one o'clock in the morning, she was sure he was asleep. She had promised that if he hadn't called or answered by two-thirty, she would go over there. He sent Joseph over there instead. "Knock it down if need be." Joseph, being a fan of Amara, said he'd do whatever.

Joseph and Logan had been at polar opposites of the argument on whether Amara was the right one for Noah. There had been years that Noah pined after the cat-eyed beauty, but she wouldn't relent and just let their love flow. She had to control every aspect and ultimately ran away. More than once, leaving Noah to lick his wounds. Everyone got tired of it, but Logan was the most vocal about how miserable Amara had made him.

Regardless, of what anyone else thought he loved her too much to give up on her and waited for her to give in. She gave in two years ago, and they've been married for a year now. He had heard that the first year can be tough on newlyweds, with the getting to know how to live together phase and all. But he and Amara seemed to be the right fit, never enough friction for him to think he'd made a mistake by giving up his freedom. No, she is who he wanted and with her is where he forever wanted to be. And Amara felt the same, easily taking on the role of wife as if she hadn't fought it vehemently for over the years. She doted over Noah while, at the same time, giving him the space she and he both needed.

"Don't you need to get back out there, dude?"

"No. I called in and asked to take some personal time. Montane went back to grab another tech."

"That's your female partner?"

"Yep."

"And you're not screwing her," Noah said with disbelief.

"She's a lesbian," Logan said simply.

"Ahhhh," Noah remarked as if that had to be the only answer for his friend not sleeping with an attractive woman.

Amara started to cry as she hung up, so Noah went to grab her.

"Come on, baby. Let's sit down."

He gathered her in his arms and brought her down with him on one of the couches.

"I'm sorry, Noah."

"Hey, none of that. You cry as much as you need to. It's okay to be upset but she is getting the best care here and I'm sure we'll hear she's okay." She nodded and sniffled before burying her face against his strong warm neck.

"You know that's why I love you, right? You are always so positive."

"I have to be in order to balance out your cynicism."

She gave him a weak, watery smile, "You're right," she agreed while snuggling deeper into his embrace.

"How's Logan?" She asked after a while.

"He'll be okay. He just wants to make sure Cami makes it."

She leaned forward and looked over at Logan as he messed around on his phone. She watched him and despite his deliberate patient movements, his jaw was ticking as if he were worried, upset and concerned about Cami as much as she. If she didn't know any better, she'd think he really cared for her friend. But it was probably the paramedic in him and he knew Cami from the wedding and a few things she and Noah had invited their friends to since they'd gotten married. Barbeques, Noah's birthday party in Vegas last December, etc. Though every time she saw them together, she had a feeling that there was a spark there.

Potential spark.

Amara wasn't sure why she felt that way when she once hated Logan when she found out he referred to her as Misery. A name that was replaced when she finally let Noah out of his anguish and married him. Now Logan was the guy she secretly rooted for because she knew he seemed sad at times and his women-chasing-ways covered it up. Both of them could use some love and wouldn't it be something if they found it together? But Cami was far from falling in love. She was barely living at this very moment. So first things first.

Mr. Douglas arrived shortly after and hugged Amara so tight that his pain was shared with hers. She started to tear up but decided not to be selfish. Cami was his daughter and this had to be worse for him after having already lost his wife. He walked over to Noah who was talking to Joseph.

"Thank you for sending your brother, son. This old man doesn't wake to the phone ringing like I used to, but it seems I need to be a lot more alert."

He turned to Amara, "Any news yet?"

"Not yet. I've been waiting and keep bugging the nurses, but they say the doctor will be out to talk to us."

Just then, a tall, lean man approached them in a white jacket. His face held no expression and anticipation kept them in suspense until he said, "She will be okay and make a full recovery. We were able to get all her vitals stabilized and she's now being sent to a room where she will be monitored before being sent to psych for an evaluation."

Seeing the look on their faces, he went on to explain that it was standard when something like this happens. They then waited until someone came to tell them that they could go see Cami in her room. They were asked not to disturb her and that the visit would be short.

They all just wanted to know what happened to her. She was the only one able to give them the answers they sought but they couldn't press and risk sending her over the edge. Amara wanted desperately to believe that her friend wouldn't try to commit suicide. It had to be something else, but what else could it have been with that bottle of pills and the alcohol? What could have sent Cami in that direction?

They spoke the day before and Cami seemed okay. Well, she seemed a little upset, but things had been that way since she was with Mr. Man. That's what Amara called him because of his apparent arrogance. He was slowly breaking Cami's beautiful uninhibited spirit bit by bit.

When Amara thought it was over between them at the wedding, she was wrong. He apparently had said and done what he needed to do to get what he wanted, and that was Cami. Amara wondered what the pull was to him? Why would Cami subject herself to the pain of being with a man who could only offer her temporary warmth, temporary loving, and temporary attention? She was his temp and he hers. Because of how Amara came to be in this world, she thought it was the craziest and most harmful behavior of Cami's and Amara had been around for many of them.

The drugs Cami had tried out, more than weed. She had been around for the drinking binges that led to Cami sharing how she didn't know how she made it home some nights. She had been around for the threesomes she participated in with couples who wanted to try something different. Since she worked as a bartender during college, she often would be propositioned. Cami had a wholesome yet seductive thing going for her. Wholesome enough to pull off being a teacher to impressionable kindergartners. Seductive enough to take anyone's husband, although Jay would be the first she actually stayed with for as long as she did.

CHAPTER FOUR

LOGAN WALKED INTO THE ROOM, almost reverently as if the person lying in the bed was of some great importance and he was worried he'd offend her with his presence. Everyone else had left out to allow her to rest and he pretended to be needing to use the restroom before heading home just so that he could peek in on her just to see if she was back to the woman he thought he knew. But she was frail and obviously didn't see herself as being important because she nearly took her own life. He didn't want to think Camille would do such a thing. The more rational option was that she had a lapse in judgement and took too much medicine and also had been drinking, not really knowing that the result could be death.

He'd seen it a few times in his line of work. Sometimes people go too far and hopefully someone is there to help save them in time. Once they are saved, they vow never to be so stupid again. Yeah, it had to have been an accident. That was the likely option. But Amara said that Camille called her upset and extremely drowsy and was saying her final good-bye. So the most realistic option was that she was not making a mistake but was, in fact, sure about what she was doing.

Looking at her now, it was hard to see Camille as anything but beautiful. Even with the dark circles under her eyes and even with her usually golden-brown skin being a little pale, she was still a sight to behold. He had always thought so. Now she looked fragile. Not full of smiles, laughs and life like he saw at the wedding. Now she was asleep and looked weak and spent. The Superman in him wanted to right her wrongs and right her world so that whatever sent her down this path was gone.

That was a dangerous place for a man to take on cases that were not his responsibility. He left before she had a chance to see that he was even there.

Two days later, after going through a series of evaluations that Camille wittingly was able to convince the doctors that she was no threat to herself or others, she finally took account of her actions that led her to be in this hospital for a psych evaluation.

It started with the question, "Did she want to die?"

The answer was yes, she did want to die but she hadn't really thought about killing herself. Not intentionally, but at that particular time, she wanted everything to go away. All the pain. All the memories of what she'd done to herself. Was that just as bad? She had to agree that it was because the result would have been the same if Amara wasn't her usual punctual and reliable self. She might not have gotten the help she needed and she'd be gone.

She looked around the sterile-looking room taking it in, until her eyes caught a burst of color. Even though there wasn't a card, Cami knew who they were from; she recognized the arrangement, the paper and the vase. In fact, she had two vases just like that one in her kitchen pantry.

The flowers were from Jay Taylor; he used to send Cami flowers all the time. But they usually were proceeded by some misunderstanding they had, some hurtful remark that he said, some planned rendezvous that he missed, or some promise he didn't keep; whatever the reason, it always spelled disappointment. She wondered how he found out she was there and wondered if he would come to see her before she was discharged, but he didn't.

Jay found out that she was in the hospital through Nicole, his newest potential Cami. She mentioned not being able to get the bracelet she ordered from Cami at a party she hosted. Nicole told Jay that she had an appointment to pick up the products at Cami's apartment but when she had arrived, someone in the building said that Cami had been taken to the hospital the night before. Jay called around and found out what hospital she was in, but they wouldn't give him any information about her condition. It wasn't until he called one of his clients he sold medical equipment to at the hospital that he found out what happened, knowing good and well that protocol was being broken by telling this information.

He met Nicole one evening at the end of one of Cami's jewelry parties. Well, he thought it would be over but there were a few lingering guests. When he made it to the hallway outside of Cami's unit, Nicole was coming out and gave him a shy smile. Her eyes were beautiful and reminded him of Cami's. All innocence and sexual allure. He had no idea why he did it, but he stopped to talk to her for a few minutes and ended up with her number. She never asked why he was heading to Cami's apartment, so he never had to explain the connection.

The fact that she didn't ask questions was huge in his book. He'd already started to phase Cami out before the incident that led her to the hospital. It wasn't that he didn't love Cami, it was partly because he loved her too much. It had gotten way too serious and because of that, he continued to disappoint her. They'd fight and then he started to feel like he was in a marriage he needed to escape. That defeated the purpose of a mistress in his opinion.

So he thought it might be time to try this again, but with someone new. It never occurred to him to just be faithful, not with Althea. She was not his dream, though at one time he thought she was, but she, like so many women before and after her, pretended to be someone else and once she got him, turned into a headache. But she was his headache and he never intended to do anything to make her turn into a migraine, so his extramarital activities were to remain a secret.

He didn't even want to think about how close he'd come to messing things up with Althea with the Cami situation. Jay couldn't risk her finding out about *all* of his games, so it was better to cut the ties with the one that was the most trouble. Cami wasn't dramatic, not really. He never had to deal with her tripping, but he knew she wanted more than he could or would ever be able to offer her. He was married and Cami knew that, but it didn't stop her from hoping for things that were hard to give her.

In the beginning, he held her far away from his heart, but somehow in all of his playing around, he actually started to care about her and love her deeply. So yeah, it became time to break things off, but he had to do it slowly at first. Less calls. Less answers. Less of everything until she started to accept less and then he could start to pull away even more. She wasn't dumb and knew that things were changing but he had an excuse – he is married. He didn't want trouble from Althea and that was true, but Nicole also needed a bit of his time too. Nicole needed to be wooed so he'd get her right where he wanted her too.

So after learning about what happened to the woman he spent almost two years sneaking around with, his first thought was to go straight to the hospital and see about her, but then he thought twice about it. Jay glanced at Althea and the set of her jaw was still tight. She was still threatening divorce over my affair with Cami and since that wasn't an option he wanted, he had to decide. If he was really going to be finished with Cami, going to see her was the wrong thing to do. Not only for him, but for Cami as well. He could only imagine what part the exposure of their relationship and Althea's calls, threats and subsequent actions to get Cami fired played in the situation. Most people could barely hold up to one of those things, but Cami endured it all. All because of him. He couldn't help but blame himself for what Cami did to herself because he told her it was over. He knew that she loved him and his words would have been devastating for her, but they had been necessary to try to put his own life back together.

But none of this history or my explanation would do any good to Cami. Her life was ruined is how she saw it. He still went home to someone and she, well, her someone was gone.

CHAPTER FIVE

CAMI HAD ONLY BEEN at her father's house recovering for a few days and she felt ready to crawl out of her skin. She felt stifled and confined with all the constant check-ups between him and Amara. She knew they meant well.

"If I didn't know any better, I would think you planned to die, Cami. Tell me I'm wrong."

Cami said nothing; she just stared at the flower arrangement that seemed out of place in the dim room. They were the bright, beautiful, Calla Lilies from the hospital. He had great taste – everything he gave her made her feel desired. That was until he stopped wanting to actually be in the relationship. Then the baubles were *shut her up* gifts. The flowers most likely meant the same thing.

But their beauty wasn't the only reason they seemed out of place. They didn't belong here because he didn't belong. He didn't belong to her. She didn't belong to him. It was over.

"You're wrong," she said finally looking into Amara's concerned eyes. There were times she wondered what she did to have such a great, caring and loving friend. Amara had her ways, but her ability to always being there when it counted was something Cami could never ignore or undervalue. No one else stayed around like that, excluding her dad. But Amara, even when upset at Cami for her antics, was still there.

"I was very broken and if I were to be honest with you, I still am. I wish I could crawl inside of a hole furnished with all necessary comforts, of course, and wait it out until everything blows over and I feel better, mended and whole. Or, I wish I could go back to before the *incident* and pretend everything is okay and pretend I'm happy when I'm really not. But some things you can't ignore, even when being oblivious, seems like the best option for survival. It's that damn wall we're stuck with."

"Now you sound cryptic, Cami, which isn't like you."

"Amara, you know the saying, *the writing is on*

the wall? Well, it's been scribbled up there in bright bold script and there's a reason some things get put there for you to see. It's because we're not supposed to ignore the message. We can't continue on the path of destruction claiming ignorance of a pending disaster when we woke up to that damn writing on the wall. We can't say there wasn't a clear message to bail out, when it's there every time you call him and he doesn't answer and every time he finally calls you, he sounds like he's obligated to keep things under control. You can't ignore the feeling of not being loved. No, the message on the wall said to me, you are not in his heart, you are not for him, and you need to move on because staying will kill you. The message was right, Amara. I almost died trying to ignore it, but I now know that the wall is always right and to never ignore that smug know-it-all bastard."

Cami thought back to all the times she ignored the writing on the wall, many times out of choice. The choice to have fun, rather than have something meaningful with anyone. The relationship she had before Jay had been the biggest sign of that. Being knocked upside your head and in your ribs were signs she could no longer ignore but decided to until that ugly loss. Losing your baby in the bathroom with Amara there to help you clean up, were signs no woman could ignore. Amara was really there through that abusive relationship.

She thought she was done with those things until Jay walked in. He was a distraction to the pain she felt most nights when she thought about how lonely she really was. How torn she had been for ... forever. Ever since her mom died and left her in this world with just her father, she had been lonely. Dad was as loving as most dads. He was there but spent a lot of time working. Cami with her wild ways and curiosities about life were too hard for him to contain with his typical straightforward answers. The emotional losses were heavy on a teenager with her spirit and eventually she fell into a destructive behavior that not many understood.

Amara saw it though and often tried to talk some sense into her as if Cami would ever listen to her goodie two-shoe friend. She loved Amara, but Amara wanted everything to fit into some sort of order and Cami knew she was far from organized or perfect. Like right now, Amara was trying to fix what was broken inside of her but what's done is done and there is no way to fix it now. The name of the game was to keep moving towards what she didn't know. Getting a job was priority number one.

"Is there anything else you need, girl?" Amara

asked her. Her cat eyes were so full of concern and pity, and Cami hated it.

"No, ladybug. You hit the road."

Amara hesitated like she had something deep to share but then she shook her head like she had to clear it. "What is it, Amara?"

"It's nothing. I just thought about something I needed to do for my husband." Her vagueness put Cami on high alert but having spent too much time in someone else's marriage already, she let it pass.

"Okay. So where are you headed now?"

Again, a pause. "The doctor and then to the grocery store to get the stuff to make Noah my mom's chicken and dumpling recipe. He's been bugging me about it since last week and since she's out on that cruise, she can't do it, so it's up to me to feed my big old baby." The dreamy look in Amara's eyes made Cami's heart ache with regret and a bit of envy that she would never share with her friend.

"When does your mom come back?"

"Saturday, so that means I have three more days to check on her house and talk to her plants–".

"Wait, what … you have to talk to her plants?"

Amara started to laugh while nodding her head vigorously. "Yes, girl. She's a trip but I admit that her plants are so healthy. Looks like a rainforest in her sunroom. She said they bring her peace and that she could use all the peace she could get in her life. Keeps her from going crazy."

Amara looked away and started to busy herself with gathering her stuff. She had struck a cord and she knew it and Cami couldn't hide it. Tears filled her eyes thinking about how she had allowed herself to crack, all over a man.

Amara's kiss to her brow interrupted those bad thoughts that were like weeds. Amara, and the love that sisterly kiss transfused, were keeping them from taking root again even though it would take a master landscaper to get rid of those nasty pesky roots that were so deep they would be impossible to reach.

"I'll call you later." Cami watched her friend leave her room, taking with her that warmth that only she radiated, and she was alone again until her dad got home from shopping. He said he had to get food if they were going to eat three square meals a day until she was able to go home and he went back to work.

Everyone's life was rearranged for her. All because of her ... again.

. . .

"*BUTTON.*" Her dad's voice seemed so far away but the constant nudging on her back dragged her out of her sleep.

When she opened her eyes and found her dad's pink-rimmed eyes looking into hers, she knew something was terribly wrong. Maybe her mom told him about Cami skipping school that day, which left her worn out from arguing with her mom.

What didn't her mom get? She was tired of school. It didn't matter that everyone said she was brilliant, she didn't like to be there all day. She would rather find something cool to get into so she spent time at Jess's house when she should have been learning something constructive. Jess had a piano and her downstairs was full of cool and unusual art pieces that inspired her to draw when she felt like it. Her mom didn't get it. So maybe her father was about to lay into her.

She had to play it cool though. "Daddy, what's wrong?" Maybe she can give him her sweet girl act and get out of a sure punishment. She was his baby girl.

He just pulled her up out of the bed into his tight embrace and his body started to shake. She realized he was crying. Something was really wrong.

"What is it, Daddy?" She asked him through the cotton of his uniform top.

"It's your mom, Button."

Cami pulled back confused. Why would he cry. Why wouldn't he just be mad?

"She's gone. She gone," he whispered.

"What do you mean she's gone?"

Cami's father didn't say anything for a while, which only made her start to cry too. When the tears had passed and he was just rocking, he explained that her mom had stopped at the convenience store to grab some bread, most likely to make lunch, and was caught in the middle of a robbery. She was shot while still holding the Roman Pride wheat bread she loved.

It had been her fault, she knew that. If she hadn't skipped school and the office didn't call her mom, her mom would have still been at work and not out there talking to Jess's mom about her daughter's truancy and its effect on Cami. She wouldn't have been at that store at that time because she would have just been getting off of work and would have went to the store that was on the way home where there wouldn't have been some kid with a gun trying to take fifty dollars from the convenience store. It was her fault her mother was dead.

CHAPTER SIX

CAMI'S FATHER had spent some time turning over in his mind all the events involving his daughter over the past few weeks. He was extremely troubled by what he'd learned, and he knew that he would need to take some time to talk to her. But being a man accustomed to leaving emotional issues to women, he didn't know where to start but knew he needed to talk to his baby girl.

Cami had been withdrawn since she came home with him. He figured some of this had to do with a man. The day Amara and Noah came with some of his daughter's belongings, he pulled Noah to the side.

Noah said that Amara shouldn't be carrying all

of that stuff even if she did insist that she could handle everything herself.

"Son, women like independence until they don't want it."

He smiled and revealed that boyish look that either got him his way or in trouble, depending on who's telling the story.

"Yeah well, Mr. Douglas, I'm learning that well."

"Good, glad you are."

He liked Noah the moment he met him. Whenever Cami would choose to have her parties at his house for the space it provided, he could see how much this young man loved his wife. It would make him remember his late wife and immediately he would be reminded of how he and Cami were left behind with the pain of her being gone.

Cami suffered, he was sure of it, but she never made a peep. Matter of fact, she became more behaved after his wife's death and that surprised him due to how rebellious she was previously. He wondered how much she was hiding from him now. It was clear that some things were hidden.

That day he asked Noah a tough question. A question that revealed he didn't know that much about his daughter.

"So, what do you know about what happened with my daughter, Noah?"

Noah looked uncomfortable and shifted on his feet like he didn't want to answer but Mr. Douglas remained focused on getting an answer.

"Amara doesn't say much really."

"I'm guessing she doesn't, but she says enough and even though women don't make sense, we are smarter than we appear. So let it out."

"It's probably over some guy ... but that's all I know. I swear."

Mr. Douglas nodded and let Noah finish bringing the things in the house.

He had figured as much. What else would drive a woman mad besides a man? Maybe children but Cami didn't have any children. So, knowing the only way to get better information was to go to her room and talk to her.

The room reminded him of his wife, Nellie because of how she had worked on each detail for her daughter; wanting it to be perfect for her personality. There were bright and muted tones mixed together, posters of the groups Cami liked at the time; Bilal from The Boys whom she had such a crush on. She begged her parents to call that hotline number so she could hear his voice say, *Hi, this is Bilal* ... Cami never changed her room after her mom died.

"Hey, Button."

He had named her that when she was born because of her adorable nose.

"Hey, Dad."

Her voice was sad, lacking all the passion he knew she used to have. Maybe she hadn't had it for a while.

How much had he missed? He wondered again.

"How are you feeling today?"

She smiled but he knew she was indulging him because she seemed to hate the constant coddling, but he didn't know what else to do.

The doctors said to be present, available for her needs, and to make sure she was socializing some. To also be patient and he had all the patience in the world since he took some time to be with her.

"I'm okay today, Dad." She really wasn't and didn't know when or if she would ever be okay but he needed to know that wherever she found herself, he needn't worry anymore. She knew enough to know she wouldn't allow things to get this bad ever again.

And he thought she would stop there like usual, but Cami surprised him when she patted the spot next to her in the bed.

"How are you today, Old Man?"

He smiled at the endearment and moved to sit down next to her on the bed. There really wasn't a reason for her to stay in the bed but it's where she'd been for the past few days.

He assumed it was a crutch. A way to say I'm sick and I need time to get better. Getting better was all he wanted for her, so he would leave her alone about the bed for a while.

"I wish I could say I'm doing just fine but you are worrying me. So, what happened? And don't tell me it's nothing and that everything is okay. Something is not right. You tried to kill yourself."

"That's not true."

"Let's be honest with each other, Button."

Cami paused and looked at her father, the only man to really love her and even if they sometimes seemed far apart, he was her father and there would never be another man to love her.

"I didn't try to kill myself, Dad. I just wanted the pain to end and I know it seems like the same thing, but it wasn't for me."

He seemed to think on that for a little while before nodding.

"When your mother died, I had moments like that, but I knew there was no one else to take care of you. Everyone else disappeared after the food was gone and the flowers dried out. It was just me and you and I had to be here for you.

"I know I couldn't give you the affection your mother gave you. She loved you so much and never wanted you to go without the love. She would always say 'that girl's free spirit might lead to loneliness but never when she's around me'. So when she was gone, and I wanted the pain to end, I just worked. Worked harder so that I could take care of you and get you that education she wanted you to have."

Cami just looked down into her lap, her hands clasped together. To some degree, she knew all of this and she never resented her father for doing what needed to be done to take care of her in the way he had. She felt responsible for her own life, good or bad.

"But now, I realized I failed you."

That made her look up.

This was not his fault.

"No, Dad. You didn't–"

"Yes, I did," he said, cutting her off. "Because whatever was bad enough that you thought you had to blot it out and almost take your life with it, I didn't see it. I haven't been here for you, but I'm here now."

Cami couldn't say anything to that. She knew it wasn't his fault. She knew that she was the only one to blame for her affliction, but the pain wasn't in the stage yet where she was ready to discuss it. The pain was still too raw to talk about. This was about more than Jay. This was about the horrible person she'd been in getting involved in things that were destructive to others and to herself. She was selfish and she couldn't live with being that person anymore. In fact, she was unable to live that way anymore. Even though her intent had not been to kill herself, almost dying was like being reborn from the fire she lit. She had become a Phoenix and it was time to emerge from the old carcass. It was time to be someone new. But that required her silencing herself, removing herself from the grasp everyone else wanted to have on her. No matter how well their intentions, she needed a moment to fly solo and breathe and only then can the company they were showering her with feel good. She just hoped they could be what she needed, not judgmental, not pressing – just there.

Her dad must have sensed her withdrawal and rather than force her to endure anymore, patted her hand and left the room. She slid down under her covers and went to sleep. Sleep didn't have pain in it, since she had long stopped dreaming.

CHAPTER SEVEN

IT HAD BEEN two weeks since Cami returned home from resting and recuperating at her father's house. How Logan knew this was through Noah. He was pitiful, asking about Cami every time he spoke to Noah, which was typically every couple of days when he'd stop by to play a game of chess and drink a brewski. After two failed attempts at prying information out of his brother, he finally just asked.

"What's going on with Cami?"

"What do you mean?" asked Noah.

"Is she doing okay? That's what I'm asking."

Noah paused in the middle of placing his piece down on the board. "Now why would that interest you?"

"Because I was the one to respond to her call."

When Noah still looked at him, piece still suspended in the air, he added, "And I usually never get to find out what happened to the people I helped once they reach the hospital. That's all."

One more look of suspicion and Noah seemed nullified and placed his piece down on the board.

"From what I understand, she is back to herself but not exactly," he said almost cryptically, which Logan picked up on.

"And what does 'but not exactly' mean?"

"Well, I think it means that physically, she's okay but emotionally, not so much. And before you ask me more questions about that, I really can't tell you. I take all I know about women from Amara. She shares and I listen and depending on what she's sharing, I try to process with male logic, which, if you haven't figured out yet, is faulty. So I have no idea how Cami really is doing, is what I'm saying."

"Why didn't you just say that?"

"I did. I've been telling you that for days now, every time you ask. I just want you to be straight about why you care so much. The Logan outside the job could care less about a woman."

"Maybe I'm turning over a new leaf."

Noah laughed. "Maybe," he said, still chuckling because Logan Graham turning over a new leaf was hysterical. "But when it comes to that one, you need to be sure you are interested in what you find on the other side."

Logan considered those words while he spent his afternoon chilling with Noah. When Amara returned from her hair appointment, he used that as an opportunity to leave. Seeing them kiss and touch didn't bother him until today. Today, he felt like he wished he had that too.

Somehow, he made it to her apartment building and was able to get in when another tenant was leaving, and without thinking about why he was drawn to coming here, he just knocked on her door when he stepped in front of it. She opened the door a few moments later, looking beautiful and surprised.

"Logan," she said, her cheeks flushed as if she were exerting herself before he arrived when in reality, she had been spending so much time alone on the couch that even the shortest distance would have blood rushing to her golden cheeks.

"Camille."

"Uh, come in." Confused by why he was there, but still not unnerved by it, she moved aside to let him in. He, also confused by why he drove there, noted how good she smelled. Like summer, sunshine and fresh air.

As she closed the door behind him, he stammered with trying to find the right words to explain him being there.

"You have a nice place," he said.

Neither of them mentioned the fact that he'd been there before or why he had.

"Thank you. Would you like something to drink, Logan?"

"Water if you have it. I mean..." He wanted to smack himself. Of course she had water.

Giggling and completely oblivious to his nervousness, she said, "It's cool. I know what you meant. Let me grab a bottle. Have a seat. I'll be right back."

He watched her retreat to her kitchen so he removed his jacket, laid it on the side of a chair and he took a seat on the comfortable sofa. He noted that she hadn't asked why he showed up yet and that relieved him. If he could get through this without having to answer the question he had no answer to, he'd be happy.

When she returned, she sat down across from him in her big arm chair and tucked feet under her legs.

"Having a good day?" She asked. This was the first time she'd been alone with Logan and his presence, though unexpected, didn't make her feel uncomfortable, she noted. She also noted that he was still fine as ever, something that never escaped her. She had just been so distracted with Jay that she didn't spend time thinking about his voice, or his large hands, or his intense and seeking eyes. She always suspected he wanted to have a fling with her at the wedding, but the timing was all wrong. She was laying into Jay for not being where he said he'd be, which was by her side.

So Logan coming to ask her for a dance was a bit irritating, but now she wondered what might had happened if she had allowed herself to think of herself at Amara and Noah's reception.

"It's been great so far. You?"

"I actually haven't done much today." It was small talk and they both knew it, but again, it didn't bother her.

Having no other small talk in him, he dealt with the elephant in the room.

"I know you're wondering why I'm here."

"I am, but I don't mind you being here," She said truthfully.

He smiled, seemingly pleased, "That's good because I don't have a good reason other than to see how you're faring." That got a small smile out of her but no eye contact. She was just that quickly reminded of the real reason why he'd come. He saw her laid out, weak and close to dying.

She fidgeted with the hem of her big T-shirt before finally looking up at him with those big light brown eyes. "I've been better, but I was a whole lot worse too."

"I can understand that." And he could. He had been in the state of limbo for a while now.

She gave him a wan smile before saying, "I'm just waiting for everyone to stop treating me with kid gloves. It's not what it looked like."

"What was it? If you don't mind me asking because you were non-responsive, Camille."

"No one else but my mother called me Camille," she said with a sad smile.

"If it's okay, I'd like to call you Camille. You have a beautiful name and Cami just doesn't do it justice."

She entrapped him with her direct stare, assessing him but he didn't flinch. He wanted her to know there were things about her that were beautiful, unique, and he noticed it from the time he met her, whether he knew to even admit that to himself.

"It's my name, so of course you can use it."

It didn't go unnoticed by him that she still chose not to answer his earlier question about what happened to her but for now, he'd let it rest and hopefully they could come back around to it.

"Have you been a paramedic for long?"

"Only a couple of years now. Well, first an EMT and a few months ago, I was promoted to paramedic."

"Do you love what you do?" She asked, seemingly interested in him.

"I do, but there are days that are harder to stomach than others."

"I can only imagine. You probably lose a lot of people before they make it to the hospital."

He chose not to respond to that. He didn't want to admit to only losing one, and then that leading to more conversation about that one person.

"Want to watch a movie?" It was a perfect retreat and neither of them had to talk about their demons.

"Sure, I have a little time to burn before I head to the station."

He settled in on the couch and she decided to sit next to him, grabbing a throw and placing it on her lap. She chose a *Marvel Universe* movie which seemed to excite him but within a few minutes, she could hear him softly snoring beside her. Smiling, she grabbed the throw and placed it on him before leaving the room to do some of her chores.

CHAPTER EIGHT

LOGAN WASN'T sure why he felt relaxed enough to fall asleep on her couch. That was not his style. As a matter of fact, even after the greatest sex he ever had, he got his happy ass up and left. He didn't sleep at anyone's house but his own, but there he was waking up an hour later to find himself covered by a cream-colored crocheted blanket and to hear Camille's humming floating in the air.

He moved the blanket to the side, did a quick stretch and got up to look for the songbird. He found her in the kitchen, where she was pulling a tray of cookies out of the oven. He watched her unencumbered and enjoyed the sight of her and her lush curves. She still hummed, unaware that he was there in the doorway of the kitchen watching her. Her voice was whimsical, almost small but still powerful enough for him to know she had a great singing voice.

Finally, she must have realized she wasn't alone. She turned from the counter and gave him a small smile.

"I hope my banging around here didn't wake you up," she offered.

"It didn't. It was just time for me to get up and out of here. I go into work soon," he said, staring at her intently.

She wasn't sure why she was suddenly filled with nerves, but here in this moment, his presence made her feel a way that she hadn't felt before. At least not with him. His broad shoulders filled the doorway. The way his brown skin glowed under the lighting had her wanting to reach out and touch it. The way his eyes, at half mast, probably from his recent nap, pulled her in and held hers. She wanted him and that bothered her because when he first arrived, she told herself that she was just happy to have someone check in on her, not someone to get into trouble with.

She had actually been feeling lonely and had been keeping herself from texting anyone, calling anyone and then her bell rang, bringing her what she needed – quiet company. He hadn't pressed her and though it was obvious he was curious about what had been going on, specifically what he saved her from, he didn't continue with the questioning.

She was usually a busy person. Spending the majority of her days with a room full of kindergartners whose energy were unmatched, made it imperative she be able to keep up. So, after a few short moments taking in his features as he slept unaware, she decided to get up and bake.

Lately that's all she'd been doing. Baking cookies, cakes, and pastries and taking them to her dad or over to Amara's. Amara hadn't complained about the baked goods the way she imagined. While Amara was what most men would label thick in all the right places, Amara herself felt she struggled with her weight. The little pudge in her midsection never went anywhere and she often lamented over how Cami could eat a house and never gain a pound.

"It's my metabolism. Besides, you're beautiful just the way you are."

And she was with her cat eyes, pouty heart-shaped lips and full fluffy hair, Amara was most men's dream. Camille was too, just a different flavor. But regardless of the compliments, Amara hated that no amount of working out got rid of the middle.

But when Amara didn't shoo the sweets away, Cami was surprised, but now she knew she had somewhere to place her baking energy. And then there was Logan, who looked like he could use a few extra meals.

Now maybe he would eat these cookies...

"These just came out of the oven. Maybe you can take them in to work with you. Maybe share with your partner. She helped you when you were here ... with me?"

She started to look away when he told her, "Don't do that. Don't ever be ashamed for needing help. We all need it. I'm just glad we got there in time."

He watched as she nodded before pushing back her shoulders to recover and this pleased him.

"And yes, my partner, Montane was with me. She'll gobble these up and any sweets you bake."

Smiling, she asked him, "But, will you?"

"I'll gobble up whatever you give me, Camille."

Her face warmed at the double meaning whether he intended it or not and she was sure she was blushing noticeably, but it didn't make him uncomfortable. Just as she allowed herself the warmth of feeling desired to take hold, the memory of how it ended the last time assaulted her.

And just like that, she felt sad and rejected again and just as her blush had, she was sure her trauma began to show on her face. She was ashamed and didn't want Logan to see her this way and hoped he'd get the hint and just leave. Instead, he decided to enter the kitchen and reached for her. This should have creeped her out. This affection from him so early on, but it didn't. In fact, as she nuzzled into his embrace, she felt what he was giving her.

Love.

It wasn't sexual. It was platonic, but it was the hug she apparently had been needing because suddenly she was shaking and crying. The kind that turned into hiccups; the kind that wet his sweatshirt. He didn't seem to mind, he just held her until the storm inside of her was over.

After a while, his voice vibrated against her ear when he said, "Like I said, never be ashamed of needing help. We all need it and I'm here whenever you need it." She believed him though she had no idea he would need to take his own advice. She knew, without a doubt, she could call on this man if she needed, and she knew that maybe she'd never ask for the help, but she would want him around. She felt it already.

He pulled away and left her standing there to

gather herself while he grabbed his jacket and started to leave. She followed him to the door and neither of them said a word as he left. It was almost like they didn't need to speak about the moment they shared. The moment when she let herself go with him.

Never had she done that. Sexually yes, with reckless abandon, but to let her fears and her hurt out with her cry, never, not with anyone around.

But she had with him.

CHAPTER NINE

THEY CONTINUED the pattern over the next few days. Actually, it had been weeks, and while Cami knew she needed to get out of the house and look for a new job, the prospect of missing out on Logan coming over for lunch, sweets and a movie was almost unbearable. So she stayed in, only rushing out to grab food supplies and hurrying back to cook and bake.

At eleven, her doorbell would chime, he'd be standing there looking like one fine ass puppy dog and she'd act like she hadn't been waiting twenty-two hours for him to show up again. Cami had been feeding Logan all of the recipes she had wanted to try with Jay, but Jay was rarely over during any meal time or he didn't stay long enough to eat anything but her, so she didn't get the opportunity.

Just thinking of what she allowed herself to go through to be with Jay upset her, but it didn't leave her with that stabbing pain anymore. More like a dull ache. She took accountability for her actions. She allowed herself to think she wasn't doing any harm by being with a married man, but she had been. She harmed a committed relationship by participating in something with him, and most of all, she harmed herself. She lost the most. She lost herself.

So, in addition to taking care of Logan, his presence became a balm to her own self-healing. She meditated when he left each day. She allowed herself to cry and she started believing that she'd be okay. She even started to see a therapist from the hospital and all of it helped.

"You're going to have to stop feeding me like this, Camille," he said this as he shoveled another forkful of her collard greens down his throat.

"You keep saying that but you keep coming over here asking what I cooked for you and don't forget the texts I get in the middle of your shifts saying *FEED ME.*"

"Stop bringing up old stuff," he said around another forkful of greens. He had already made the baked chicken with gravy disappear. The only sign there was anything else on the plate were the scrape marks left by his fork.

"Well don't start nothing, won't be nothing," she responded with sass.

"Whatever I start, I finish. Keep that in mind," he said while stopping long enough to flush his food down with water.

She had long finished eating the small portion on her plate and only stayed seated to enjoy watching him eat her food.

But his last words made her think about him eating more than her food. She and Logan had long since arrived at a place where it was clear that they were into each other. While she was far from the place where she felt like she had it all together, she no longer felt she had to hide from her burgeoning feelings. All that stopped Cami from making any moves was Logan not making a move. That made her unsure. If he wanted her, wouldn't he let her know?

Besides, what would happen after they did make moves on each other? Would they be able to keep doing this friendship thing they had perfected? They both pretended that the only thing he was coming for was some apple pie and ice cream. Would they have to start acting like a real couple? Would they have to come out to their friends, who were already curious about what was going on with the visits.

In fact, Amara's question was, "Why does he need to see you at all? Noah can update him on whether you're alright since you claim that's why Logan is here every day."

Amara's smile bothered Cami but seeing that she wanted to hide just how often Logan was visiting and why she was beginning to love his visits, she avoided addressing it. He had started to nap there, even sleeping in the bed, with her often waking up on his chest or in his arms. That alone wreaked havoc on her hormones. She was wet each time she woke up in his arms and once she'd awaken, she felt him hard against her bottom. She was tempted to rub against it and start something she desperately wanted to finish but she was deathly afraid of rushing it. So she would lie still and pretend it wasn't there and eventually his breathing would change and he'd realize their position. There would be a moment of hesitation like he was deciding what to do with his hard-on and then she'd feel him retreat and either turn the other way or get out of bed.

But the other day, he'd done something different. He leaned into her. His hand traveled over her hip and then up to her side and around to her stomach. It stayed there. Cami's heart was thumping so hard she was sure he would have felt it. She held her breath just to keep from moaning. Tentatively, his hand traveled up further to just beneath her breasts where her nipples were already in tight peaks. If only he would touch them is what she was thinking, what she was yearning for, and then he did it. His hand came up to cup one and then the other, before alternating with pinching each tip. He kissed the side of her neck as she finally released her moan and rubbed her ass against his groin. Her insides were warm, her core wet, and she was ready. Right as she thought they'd move forward, his phone went off signaling it was time for him to leave for work. He muttered a curse and pulled away.

When he left, he didn't mention what they'd been close to doing and neither did she when she placed a kiss against his hard cheek and whispered, "Be safe, Logan."

CHAPTER TEN

SINCE LOGAN WAS off for the next two days, instead of giving into the temptation to simply lay around with Cami and binge-watch season four of *Star Wars: The Clone Wars*, which had become their latest addiction, he decided to finally stop running from his mother.

It was Sunday afternoon. Logan glanced at the clock on the cable box and knew that at that very moment, his mother was cooking dinner fried chicken, macaroni and cheese, collard greens, creamed corn, candied yams, jambalaya, red beans and rice, biscuits, and sour cream pound cake, and he was hungry. Even though it was usually just the four of them, his mom always cooked enough to feed an army.

Cami was a great cook and an even better baker. Since he hadn't been going to his parents' house for Sunday dinner, she had been keeping him full, fat, and happy. He patted his stomach and thought that she was keeping him too full and he was getting too fat and it was time for him to either push back from the table or committed to working out. Earlier that morning when Cami woke up, she said that she had a full day of job hunting and she would get with him later that evening which made it easy for him to finally go home.

He had been avoiding his mother for months now, and it was well past time to man up and face her. Logan got up from the couch and headed towards the shower knowing that if he went to Sunday dinner, that wouldn't be an opportunity to avoid his mother. He'd have to contend with her.,

*A*s he stood there hoping the water would wash away all of his worries, he thought about dinner and how he could make things go the way he needed to avoid the topic that he was sure everyone wanted to have with him. And him being the topic, Logan knew that it would be a daunting task to say the least.

Like most mother's, Andrea was very nurturing, a bit nosy, and always willing to jump right in and meddle in any situation. But she meant well. Then

there was his younger sister, Doreen. She has always
been his pest, but she was his kid sister, even at the
age of 26, and he loved her in spite of her annoying,
irritating and sometimes exasperating ways. The
only respite that he would have would be his father,
Mark. Though he loved his son dearly and like his
wife, knew something serious was going on with
Logan, his father made the decision to take a more
hands-off approach. If Logan needed him, he'd be
there. He could dodge his mother's questions and
knew that his dad would jump in and get his mother
off his back if things got too thick. His line would be,
let the boy be, Andrea. Logan would give him that
'get your wife' look. The problem, as always, would
be Doreen. She was single but dating nobody in
particular, which Logan attributed to her being
annoying, irritating and exasperating. That meant
that Doreen was often alone at family functions and
that quite simply gave her plenty of time to
bother him.

Even though Doreen was often solo, Logan
always came alone because he didn't usually trust
women enough to get close to them for long. But
Camille was very quickly becoming the exception.
They were friends who were taking their time
getting to know each other. Logan was drawn to

everything about her. From her golden-brown skin to her full fluffy hair, to her soft kissable lips that he loved feeling against his. Even her eyes, almost an amber brown, sparkled when she looked at him. She entrapped him with everything about her and not just the physical. She was beautiful inside. Nothing but joy, light, and a free spirit bundled up inside a beautiful woman.

But, in the midst of all that was great about Camille, he knew that she had a hard time and at one point her spirit was hampered, even crushed, and Logan was in no way interested in rushing her out of her healing process. So instead, he is being a friend. Besides, from his past experiences with women, he knew to go slow and keep it casual and keep a little distance between them.

He had to laugh at himself because he was doing the opposite. He could tell that Camille was growing increasingly comfortable with having him around. Without either of them really noticing it, they had eased into a comfortable routine. To his surprise, it was working for him because it was so out of character for him. Either before or after his shift, Logan had got into the habit of going over and watching TV with her. Since he generally didn't sleep well because his dreams were haunted by old ghosts, on the nights when he would drop by after his shift, he would often fall asleep. It was the same whenever she'd come over which wasn't often though he was open to it happening more and more. Logan was amazed at how comfortable he was with her in his space.

The proof of his comfort was that he allowed her to just be there with him and they'd spend time together. Normally, when women came over, they came for one purpose and one purpose only and since that purpose wasn't conversation, they'd leave once that purpose was accomplished, and that was fine was him. But Camille was different from every other woman that he had ever known. She seemed to like and understand his quiet company and the spurts of laughter they shared. To him, Camille was open-minded and nonjudgmental. And since he was the same type of person, he had no problem giving her the room to heal and grow to like him more deeply. So far, neither of them had been pressed for anything and that allowed them to flow freely.

When Logan arrived at the house, his mom grabbed him up and held on to him so tightly that his dad had to pry her off of him. "Give the boy some room to breathe, Andrea. He just got here."

"It been so long since my baby boy has come to

join us for Sunday dinner. I am just happy to see him, Mark."

"Well, look what the cat dragged in," Doreen said coming out of the kitchen. "There must not be any sporting events, friends to help or lives to save for you to grace us with your presence."

"How you doing, Doreen?" he said and hugged his sister as his mother went back in the kitchen to finish cooking. Doreen was beautiful and looked just like their mother but where his mother wore her hair in a bob style that she still dyed dark brown, Doreen often wore her hair in a ponytail.

"I'm fine. Wishing I could be like you and skip Sunday dinner for a month and be able to waltz in here like it was no big deal," Doreen said and Mark shook his head and went to sit down to watch the *Steelers* and *Jaguars*.

Choosing to ignore her comment, Logan followed his father into the living room and sat down with Doreen right on his heels. "What's the score?" he asked hoping that she would go in the kitchen with mom, but Doreen flopped down on the couch next to him.

"Eleven – three, *Jaguars*."

"Get out of here."

"*Jags* got a good defense and capitalized on the Steelers turnovers," Mark said.

"We'll pull it out, we always do," Logan said, recalling the day when no matter how far down the *Steelers* were, you always had the feeling that they would come back to win.

"Those days are dead. They used to be like that, but now ... it's a nail-biter every week."

"Hush, little girl," Mark said as the ball was snapped and all three leaned forward in anticipation of a big play.

"Dinner's ready!" Andrea shouted from the kitchen, but she couldn't be heard over the shouting in the living room.

"That's what I'm talking about," Logan said and fist-bumped his dad. "Seventy-five-yard touchdown run."

"That reminded me of Marcus Allen," Mark commented.

"Super bowl run against the *Redskins?*" Logan asked.

"You know it."

"A little before my time, but I've seen highlights. And yeah, it was a great run."

"Who is Marcus Allen?" Doreen asked, and the

men laughed at her as they got up and headed toward the dining room.

Over dinner, there was the usual chitchat. As Doreen took up all the air in the room as she talked about what was going on with her job, her friends, their lifestyles and way more information about whomever she was or wasn't dating. That was fine with him, but each time he glanced in his mother's direction, he could tell that she was just waiting for Doreen to shut up so she could ask him the same question that she'd been asking for months. Although she was very interested in hearing about Doreen's love life, because to her dismay, neither of her children are settled down enough to give her any grandchildren. It was something that she hoped would change starting with her son.

"So," Andrea started the second Doreen's fork was in her mouth. "How's Shayna? I haven't heard you mention her in a while. The two of you are still working together?"

"Yes, Ma. And she's fine."

"Is everything all right at work?"

"Yes, Ma, everything is fine. You know that I just got a promotion, so there are some challenges as I learn some of the politics, but other than that, things are good," Logan said and hoped that she would drop it right there but knowing she wouldn't.

"Well, something is bothering you."

"Andrea," Mark said in a cautioning tone.

"What? All I'm saying is that I am his mother and a mother knows when something is wrong with her babies."

"Yeah, you dropped him on his head way too many times when he was a baby," Doreen laughed.

"At least I didn't wet the bed until I was nine," Logan shot back.

"That was low," Doreen said.

"It was, son. Apologize to your sister."

"Sorry."

"So what's wrong with you?" Andrea said, getting right back to her interrogation.

"I'm fine, Mom, really. Like I said, with the promotion, I just got a lot on my plate."

"I can understand that," Andrea said, but she knew her son and knew that it was more than that. "But you need to take some time to take care of yourself. There is no shame in reaching out for help if you need it and who better than the people who love you."

"Ma, I'm going to say this one more time, I'm fine. There is nothing going on with me, so I don't need to reach out to anybody because I don't need any help," he said to his mother in a tone that he thought was disrespectful. The look on Andrea's face said that she thought so too. "I'm sorry, Ma. I didn't mean to be disrespectful, but I am fine. I am happy, in fact, I met someone and though we are taking it slow, we are spending a lot of time together." He didn't really think about it, just spoke, knowing that whatever was happening with him and Camille wasn't serious enough to mention yet. But it might help his mother lay off of him.

"Probably just another air-headed floozy," Doreen quickly quipped.

Logan looked at his sister. "Actually, she's a teacher," he said, not wanting to go into any of the details about Camille's life, especially given that she was currently out of a teaching job.

"So, where is it written that teachers can't be floozies?" Doreen asked.

"You can be so annoying sometimes," Logan said.

"Thank you, big brother. I've been working on being your annoying little sister for years," she said.

"I think you got it down pat, baby girl," Mark chimed in.

"When do we get to meet her?" Andrea asked as

visions of holding her grandson or daughter flashed in her mind's eye.

"I don't know, Mom. We are so far from meeting the family right now," Logan said knowing that he had met her father and that was pretty much all the family that she had.

"Well, I still want to meet her."

"Let the boy be, Andrea. He just said that they aren't like that," Mark said.

"I know what he said, but I would still like to meet her. The last girl you brought over here was Sandra Thomas," she said, and Logan just looked at her.

"Sandra Thomas?" he paused and thought back. "I was in eighth grade," he said and everybody laughed.

"That's how long it's been," Andrea said. "I think that you should invite her to have dinner with us next Sunday."

"I don't know about all that."

"Yeah, Ma, you should be glad that he showed up for dinner and not push it." Doreen laughed. "If you do, it might be three more months before he graces us with his presence," she said and that ended the conversation. After that, Mark got up and went back to the game and Doreen began clearing the table.

Andrea sat there for a few moments looking at her son. She wasn't sure if the story of the new woman was true or if it was just to get her off his back. She didn't know but stood up and began clearing the table knowing that she would get to the bottom of whatever was going on with her baby boy.

CHAPTER ELEVEN

CAMI KNEW she had avoided his calls long enough. She knew what the calls were about because this is what they did. Regardless of how much she had believed his words when he cruelly ended everything, they shouldn't have even had been together. She knew this would happen. They would fall into that familiar pattern of him calling to ask a question and she would be cold at first and he would chip away at that ice with his concern and his short-lived consistency and then they would be back together doing the things they did and then it would change again.

For the worse.

He would start to become inconsistent and blame it on his wife; her needs, her wants, and what he had to do to keep her happy. None of it had to do with Camille, the woman he was supposed to be head over heels in love with. Not once would he ask her what it would take to continue their arrangement. No, it was always about his wife.

Why didn't he give *her* what she needed since her needs were so important? It never made sense and now that she had been healing, she understood.

Those were lies.

Lies men told to keep you in your position of loving them while they weren't free to do what they wanted. She was never to benefit from the arrangement and she had wasted so much of her time. She knew that there were many wives that hated her kind. Some of them were, in fact, her kind at one time.

Didn't they remember loving a man that was wrong for them? Wanting to give him things that he wasn't getting with the one who seemed to have him shackled.

She didn't deserve anyone's sympathy— she knew that. She had been dead wrong for loving this particular man who was married and had a beautiful daughter that she had once had the pleasure of teaching. She also had been human and fell into the same selfish trap as lots of others had, have and will fall into.

She just wasn't that woman any longer. She was healing. Love was helping her heal. Love that she had with a man that didn't have to hide her. He was slowly and surely becoming a good reason to forget about Jay. Jay would always want what he wanted but never want to give her what she wanted or needed.

Logan was giving it to her without her having to beg for it. He was just there. He smiled at her with his eyes and his lips. His whole face said he was happy to be with her. He held her hand in public. He called her for no reason at all but to hear her voice and he was never in a rush to get rid of her. Even her most mundane task of the day was something he seemed to care about. He was there. She worried it was too good to be true.

Cami remembered those days in the beginning with Jay. It was perfect and so was he. Once he had her where he wanted her, he started to slough at it all and she was left waiting. But Logan had no reason to be that man with her.

Camille picked up her phone and looked at the time to make sure it was within the appropriate time to call him. She dialed his number that she had yet to forget despite erasing his contact information from her phone. She had erased all of his ignored calls too just so she didn't have to see the number on her phone.

"Cami."

His voice had lost some of its potency; no longer making her smile. She just stared off into space until her gaze landed on her vanity. The same vanity where she'd taken the pills and nearly killed herself.

"Are you there?"

"Yeah."

"Oh, okay. What's going on?"

"Nothing much. Just returning your calls. What do you want, Jay?"

He seemed to think on that for a while, pausing like he couldn't understand her cool tone and words. She couldn't understand why he wouldn't understand.

"I wanted to see how you were doing, Cami."

"I'm fine. I thought you never wanted to hear my voice again."

Jay didn't think it would be like this. He figured by the time he started to call her again, she would have softened up a bit. Yes, he had meant everything he said that day, but he was known for his temper, especially when it came to her. She was everything his wife wasn't. Challenging, extremely intelligent, not that his wife wasn't *smart*. Cami had a brilliance about her that stirred something in him and made him want to talk to her about everything and nothing.

Well maybe not nothing since time was always limited and that was where frustration came in. He didn't have time for a real relationship with her but that's all she wanted. Sex with her was amazing. He had time for that every day of the week if he could find the excuse. But sitting around laughing and watching TV or listening to her, that took up too much time when he needed to be in other places. The contradiction of what he wanted and what he could actually do had made things unbalanced. He couldn't be what he wanted or she wanted so he started to check out of what they were doing. Plus, he was never looking for anything permanent anyway, is what he told himself.

And then there was Nicole.

Nicole Carter was new in his arrangement, but she fit in because her needs were minimal. He could call in between appointments or on the way home and she knew not to ask for more. She wasn't as brilliant, nor as beautiful. But she would do in a pinch and since Thea was upset all the time, a pinch was needed often. But he missed Cami.

He gave her his silence for a moment and then sighed, thinking about how to play this.

"You know me. I say a lot of things, but it never lasts."

"I do know that. I know that more now than ever. We didn't last either."

"What we have will never go away, Cami. You and I both know that."

"I'm surprising myself by admitting this, but you're right. There will always be a part of you within me. It's just not a big part anymore. You killed that."

"So, I'm the only one to blame? You did no wrong?"

"I did wrong. I should have never gotten involved. I broke a trust with the school and with Ali. I ruined a lot of things for myself. So yeah, I did wrong. But if you're asking whether I'm to blame for your behavior towards me? Hell no. When we started, we were both in it … and it should have ended the same way. Communication and respect should and could have been given. But you know what, that doesn't matter anymore."

His long pause was filled with anger. She could

feel it because she knew him. All that time they had together was not just about sex, it was about everything and she knew this man as well as his wife knew him. That was why Althea had set out to ruin her because that woman knew that her husband was invested in this relationship and not just slinging his rod. And though he would probably always cheat, what he had with Cami was more than that. Everyone knew it who watched from start to end.

After a moment he asked her, "Why doesn't it matter?"

"Because we're over, we're done. That's what you told me, and I've accepted it. Enjoy your evening, Jay."

CHAPTER TWELVE

"MIGHT AS WELL MAKE IT TWO," Noah said when Logan reached in the fridge to grab another *Heineken*.

Logan looked out of the open kitchen at Noah like he was crazy. "Who do I look like, the butler or somebody? Get your own, dude."

"Why it gotta be like that?"

"It doesn't." Logan laughed and handed Noah the bottle as he passed him to sit on the sofa.

"I was about to say that's what's wrong with some people, never want to do nothing for anybody, but thank you."

"You're welcome. But you're wrong," Logan said before taking a swig.

"What am I wrong about?"

"People don't want to do anything for themselves. They'd much rather have somebody do it for them."

"That may be true, but there are some things we can't do for ourselves." Noah said and moved his rook. "We can't give birth to babies. We want a child, we must get a woman."

"Whoa, bruh. I don't want any babies." Logan moved his queen and took Noah's bishop and looked up at Noah. "Do you?"

It took a long time for Noah to answer because he had to consider his answer. There was a time when his answer would have been an immediate no. And anyone who knew him, knew there was a time he couldn't be responsible for any life form, not even a plant, but Amara made him a better man. A better person and one day very soon, a great father. "Maybe one day," he said mysteriously. He moved a pawn while avoiding any more talk about babies. "Check."

"I did not see that," Logan said and scratched his head.

"We usually never do," Noah said cryptically.

"You talk to Don?" He asked Logan after a while.

"Not since Keisha put him out. He was trying to move up in here, but I wasn't having that. Don can lay up on Keisha all he wants, but everybody that lives here gotta work. That's all I'm saying. He can't keep a job long enough to move in with me."

"I think that's by choice."

"What? Don not keeping a job? That is a choice he makes. And I'll be honest with you. I have little to no respect for a man that chooses to lay up with a woman and not work. How is she going to have any respect for him?"

"That's the worst thing in the world to live with a woman that doesn't respect you. It gives her a right to talk shit because she's paying the cost to be the boss."

"A man needs to contribute or take care of it all if he's going to get any respect."

"I went out and made it on my own. Nobody had to leave anything to me for me to make it."

"Yeah, Noah, but that's because you're one of the smartest people I know. And even with that, wouldn't it have been easier for you to make it if somebody had left you some money?"

"Yeah it would, but my father is fifty-six years old and still gets up and hits the clock every day."

"So does my father." Logan laughed, "I was just telling Camille the other day how my father still has to pick up, carry and empty trash and recycling containers into that truck every day."

"Camille? This somebody new?"

"No," Logan said quickly and laughed an uncomfortable laugh. "Cami."

He was really ready to tell Noah about him and Cami and ... whatever it was that was going on between them.

"I didn't know that you and Camille were cool like that." Noah laughed. "I didn't even know that was her name. All I've ever known her by is Cami."

"Yeah, Camille's her name."

"So what's up with that?"

"What's up with what?"

"You and Camille."

"Nothing. We are really just friends," Logan said and thought about the kiss they shared the night before, knowing that calling them friends was a lie. The way his hands found their way into her hair and hers reached for his shoulders to pull him closer. Their tongues down each other's throats while their bodies moved against each other in a way where just a few moves could have them naked and he'd be inside of her. Friends or not, he felt they both wanted something more and were so close to getting it the other day. He was beginning to get rock hard thinking about it.

"All you have is friends, Logan."

He thought about that and thought about how the two of them would never move past this stage if he didn't do something about it. She appeared to be over ole dude and she also appeared to have her head on straight. He knew he wanted her. The way she smelled. The way she looked at him with those big brown eyes and soft pink lips. She was ready for him to make a move, so he decided to head over there after making a call.

"You up?"

"Yeah."

"I want to come over."

"Why, everything okay?"

"Yeah, but I need to see you. Now."

She said she'd be waiting for him when he got there, and she was. She wore only a T-shirt. Actually, it was one of his medic shirts he left over there one night and he told her she could keep it because he had many. But he only had one of her.

When Camille saw Logan standing there in her doorway waiting for her to move aside and let him in, she knew why he was there. In fact, she knew when he called at that hour. She had been wanting him too. To act as if she hadn't been touching herself to the vision of him inside of her would be lying to herself and she was beyond lies. She was living in the light.

He turned her on.

Every day they grew closer. The woman in her wanted him. And every day she took time to heal, she became more comfortable with the idea of them becoming more than just friends though she was in no rush to define whatever they were and wherever they were headed.

The thing about starting off as friends is not being sure if taking the plunge was going to put the friendship at risk for ruination. There was plenty of chemistry between them. But they had that slow game thing happening that was only solidified by all the interests they shared and participated in over the months.

So here they were, finally looking at each other in a way that said they were about to move to another level. Cami, for her part, was excited and ready. Logan was more than ready. But both were curious about what lie ahead. Though Logan had always had a humor about him and that was in each interaction, in this moment, there was no smiling. His eyes burned hot. And suddenly she felt shy.

What did she get herself into, was her thought?

But then he kissed her bare shoulder before

pulling back to look at her again. Then he leaned back in to steal a kiss from her lips and pulled back again, leaving her eyes still closed and her lips still puckered for more attention from him.

So he was going to tease her, she figured out.

There was a time where she would have aggressively taken the dick she wanted but this time, she knew that allowing him to lead was to her benefit.

She warmed under his scrutiny feeling the warmth and wetness leak from the crease of her lips. Their mouths met again, their kiss growing wild and more intense, tongues and lips touching and drawing out moans from each of them.

He pulled the T-shirt up over her head and it revealed the rest of her. She was a goddess and he would praise her and pay tribute to her each time he was with her.

He started with her neck and sucked her there where her pulse beat against his tongue. After he took her to the couch, he moved to the tips of her breasts. They were hard and big, and he lavished the sable tips with flicks and suckles.

She leaned back on the couch in surrender. He moved down to the floor to get in position to devour her. He began moving his lips down the concave of her belly, admiring her smooth skin and soft curves.

Her scent was intoxicating as well and when he opened her thighs, the fleshy golden skin was already drenched from the sweet core of her. He planned to wait it out, tease her there but shit, he couldn't. He opened up her lips and pulled her to his hungry mouth. His sucked on her like she was the sweetest fruit.

Her hands grabbed at his shoulder, trying to avoid doing the inevitable but failing. She finally reached for his head and pushed herself against his lips and his tongue. She was unable to contain hiding her need for him to take all of her. She exploded and screamed his name a moment later.

From his kneeling position on the couch, he pulled her to him so she was astride him, her back to the couch. Her body came down on his and enveloped him in her drenched opening.

She was warm, she was wet, she was tight, and she was moving on him with skill and precision.

If he wasn't careful, this would be a quick ride and he intended to have her for a long while. But as she began to bounce, and her flesh pulled him in and out of her, he then grabbed the globes of her ass into his hands. How long he had didn't matter.

His lips moved to her earlobe as she moaned, then to her sweet-scented neck. Then he pulled a nipple into his mouth and that made all the plans go to dust. She was shattering around him as her wet warmth began to catch and release, milking him. He couldn't hold back if he tried and he did try. But he failed and fell apart right along with her. He pulled her head into his chest, too afraid to let her see him freak out. Never had he cum so fast. Never.

Who was this woman, he thought?

Your woman.

CHAPTER THIRTEEN

HE'D BEEN LYING in bed on his back with his head cradled in the palms of his hands, staring up at the ceiling as if it held wisdom for how to find true peace. If there was some sort of magic to either make him forget Camille so he'd be free from the torment of her smile and her touch, he wished it would hurry up already. Or maybe he wished he knew how to handle the goodness that was her and not crush her under the weight of his demons.

The other night, he had been in that sleep. The kind of sleep that never left him feeling rested because it was filled with visitors from his not so distant past. They wanted him to fix the outcome that plagued him even during his waking hours.

He couldn't save her. He couldn't save the situation no matter how hard he tried. He had tried many times in his fitful dreams that usually left him with beads of sweat and his heart pounding like he'd ran a marathon. He went to look out the window at some vacant space until he could calm himself enough to either lie back down or do something constructive like working out.

Pumping iron helped him to clear his mind from those visitors long enough to make it through a shift. It was a medication he had started to need more and more to appear to have it all together. But he was far from having things under control and that's what bothered him. Living like this was fine for him. He could handle the pressure.

But Camille was fragile. She almost gave up on life, even if it were a mistake, over some joker who twisted her heart as if it wasn't the rarest, most beautiful gift she could ever bestow on a mortal. Her love was freedom but consuming to his soul all at once. It made no sense to him. He wanted it all but he also wanted to run hard and fast from it because it was too good. She was too good for him.

Being wrapped up in her, in her laughter, her play, her arms, in between those golden thighs ... He had to wonder why anyone would toy with it. He sure as hell didn't, which was a departure from his devil-may-care attitude he'd executed with the countless nameless women before her.

She was for him. She was really designed for him. But not the current him, the him that used to be whole. The one who would have been able to hold the woman in his arms while she snoozed without scaring her to shit because his demons were playing around in his dreams. The him, she wouldn't give a concerned look to, or try to help him calm down when he could see she was shaken and unsure of whom she lied down with. He wasn't right for her but she was right for him.

Torture. If magic existed to make this ache go away, it needed to come now.

But as she shifted in the bed beside him, her warmth cloaking him in her sleep-filled peace, he began to wonder if she was torturing him at all. To her, he can become a salve to her pain, a savior and maybe she was to him also.

But there wasn't enough of her to make him forget the pain of that call. The call that dispatched him to the house of a frequent flyer. No one could have prepared him for what he saw when he arrived. His patient, the routine domestic call, was dead. Shot to death. He had tried so many times to encourage her to leave as she refused treatment, but she refused to leave.

"They call you Angel, right?" Well, Angel, just know that I'm going to be fine. One day he'll find something else to be angry at and leave me alone."

He'd seen enough on the job to know that evil men and women never got tired of doing vile things, they just kept right on going.

But he shouldn't have been using his precious time focusing on that. In a few hours, he would be working another twelve-hour shift and would be without her. So instead, he woke her with a kiss. She stirred and mumbled something incoherent but turned to lay on her back to give him access to all that he was gorging himself on.

Before long, her legs were open and he was sliding himself deep inside. Her sleepy eyes focused on his. Her hips moved from beneath him, catching his rhythm, pulling him into her depth and into her love. He felt lost and then found and before long, they were both crying out for mercy.

CHAPTER FOURTEEN

CAMILLE HAD A THING FOR WATER, so he decided to take her on a real date where they'd spend time getting to know each other in a real and meaningful way. She was a different woman from the one he met in Barbados and she was far away from the lifeless woman he rushed to the hospital six months ago. If they were to have any semblance of a future, he had to get to know the woman she was becoming. So, with her preference for aqua, he took her to Riverfront Park on the Southside of town and they sat on a bench munching on the deli sandwiches they stopped to grab on the way.

At the Southside Works in Pittsburgh's South Side neighborhood, a former steel mill barge dock has been converted to a riverfront park in an innovative project that straddles a railroad tunnel and over-comes a forty-foot drop in elevation to provide access to the Monongahela River.

The park provided a welcoming link to Pitts-burgh's "creative class" who lived, worked and shopped at the Southside Works. Switchback terraces connect upper and lower plazas to create an exciting outdoor public space for recreation, relax-ation and special events.

"Do you know what I like most about water?"

She had stopped chewing on her pastrami and Swiss sandwich and was wiping her mouth as she looked out at the river water. He loved listening to her voice. It was whimsical, lyrical almost and so peaceful that he often yearned to feel her stroke his head with her slender fingers while she whispered words of love to lead him into a peaceful restful sleep. One that he hadn't had in months.

"What is it?"

She loved how intent on her words he was when-ever she spoke. It was like whatever she had to share was the most important thing he wanted to hear. She couldn't ever remember a man being that way with her.

Jay would often allow her to talk for long periods of time without adding a word. After a while, she realized he didn't have anything to say because he wasn't listening to her and checked out.

"WATER DOESN'T WANT ANYTHING," she finally answered. "It doesn't need anything either. It's self-sufficient but what it gives us is invaluable. We rely on it, but what does it need from us?"

He thought about that for a moment.

"Do you want to be someone that doesn't need anyone?"

That he hit the mark on the emotions she had been keeping bottled up without her having to lead him there was unsettling, but she wouldn't let him know that.

"Needing someone only leads to disappointment. I learned that the hard way."

He sensed that sadness that she worked hard to rid herself of slipping into their relaxing outing and decided to change that.

"Come on. Let's take a walk."

They threw their garbage away in a nearby receptacle and started along the lower trail alongside the bike trail. "I like water because it keeps my ass clean," he remarked.

She stopped walking and looked at him seriously.

"Yes, the ass being clean is pretty important. Anything powerful enough to clean yours deserves worship." Then they both started to crack up.

"Seriously though, I understand what you mean and I'm happy you're here with me, Camille."

Not for the first time, she shivered at the sound of her name coming from his lips. It was like he was being possessive and she liked it. Being claimed by him. He didn't like the abbreviated version of her name she preferred everyone call her. Matter of fact, many people had no idea her name was Camille.

"I'm happy to be here with you, Logan."

He took her hand in his and they continued on the trail that they shared with other park-goers and a team of ducks that were scouring for any bread people tossed out for them. Some of those ducks looked like they needed a diet if they planned to swim away in a crunch but what did she know.

She wasn't the expert on duck diets. She wasn't an expert on Logan either. She knew that being in his presence was like a balm she so dearly needed but again, she didn't want to need anyone or anything but water, air and lots of great food.

"So what are your plans tomorrow?" he asked.

"I actually have an interview."

"For real? That's great, Camille. What time is it?"

"At eleven. So, I'm going to spend tonight and the morning going over some questions I think they'll ask me."

"That's a good idea. What's the job?"

"Day Care Teacher." She sounded forlorn and he knew why. She had a master's degree in Elementary education and had five years of classroom teaching behind her and she was considering a job at a day care.

"That should be interesting," was all he could say. But he could do a lot more. He pulled her down the small hill closer to the riverbed and held her close to him, placing gentle kisses to her brow. "You're like the water, Camille. You are strong enough to do all that you need to do and no one can stop you. Even if there's a dam, eventually it will break under your pressure, but not you under it. Okay?"

She gifted him with a watery smile before leaning up to kiss his lips.

"Is that you, Cami?"

His voice was like the sound of a scratched record.

She turned and there he was with beautiful little Ali. The man she'd spent two months trying to expel from her heart. And how convenient that he'd bump into her here with the new man who was quickly replacing any old feelings or feelings of sadness.

"Ms. Douglas," Ali screamed while Camille watched her little legs work hard to get to her most favorite teacher that she missed.

Cami bent down just as Ali rushed into her arms and held her tight. The smell of honeysuckle in her hair brought tears to her eyes. All innocence, sweetness and light, she had no idea what a calamity her father was in her life.

Cami pulled back and smiled at her ex-student and marveled at the changes her face went through. In just a few months, she looked a little older and her two front teeth were now permanent. No longer the snaggletooth Ali.

Cami stood and faced the man that almost took her soul when he left and noted that he was still as handsome today as he was the first day they talked. It just no longer mattered what he looked like, what he smelled like, what his voice sounded like in her ear as he talked game about a future they would never have. She was over it.

Logan noticed immediately how Camille started to clam up in the presence of the man whose smile was much too sly and familiar with his woman. She had gone from relaxed and mellow – just the way he liked her and wanted her to be all of the time, to smiling down at the little girl she called Ali with noticeable tension.

"Hi, baby girl," she said to the little girl who was now clinging to Camille like she was her best friend.

"I'm doing just fine, Ms. Douglas ..."

Logan tuned out the rest of the chatter and focused on the man that was watching Camille like she was meat that he wanted to eat. And then the brother looked over at him like he just noticed him.

It got quiet and he looked over at Camille who was looking back and forth between them and he wondered whether there would be an introduction.

Just as the thought entered his mind, she said, "Logan, this is Jay. Jay meet Logan."

He knew that she did the right thing not placing a title there because there wasn't one. At this point, they were only friends. Friends that made love occasionally and enjoyed each other's company. He had yet to define anything between them and while she didn't seem to be pressed for a commitment, he somehow felt he should be giving it to her.

Jay looked between both Cami and Logan and they both seemed to be waiting for a reaction. He had a reaction all right, but not anything he would let them in on.

How was it that she had moved on from him already? That had never happened in between their breaks before. She looked good too. There was an inner glow to her that he didn't ever recall being there before and it made her even more appealing. By the way dude was eyeing him, he pretty much figured it was an inner glow reserved for him.

"So Jay, it was nice seeing you, but we will be going now." Logan knew enough to know that this way not what Jay wanted but the only way for this to go down smoothly was if he stepped in.

"Yeah, if we don't leave now, we'll miss more than the credits, babe." Yeah, he was laying claim. Shit, it was long overdue.

She gifted him with one of her smiles. The smile that slayed him each time she gave it and then she squatted in front of Ali who watched the strange adults without missing a beat.

"I want you to make sure you keep being a big girl for your new teacher, Mrs. Ledermann. Okay?" Camille had teacher buddies that still filled her in on the politics of the school even though hearing it was painful. They still were teaching and she was not. She missed her kids very much.

"I will." She looked as sad as Cami felt but was mature enough to not throw a tantrum.

"Thanks for bringing her over to say hello, Jay," Cami said as she stood to face him again.

"I didn't seem to have much choice in it, Cami. She loves you, you know that."

What hung in the air for all of them to hear was that so did Jay. Cami knew it and so did Logan, which made him clench his jaw and take Cami's hand. Such blatant disrespect of another man put everything into perspective for Logan. No one said another word. Cami just held his hand tighter and turned with him to the dirt path that would take them back to his parked car.

They didn't talk on the way to the car and Camille thought it was because Logan was upset. In her mind, he had to be upset because seeing Jay was just a reminder of everything she was working hard to leave behind her. Matter of fact, she had left it behind. Didn't he know?

Logan wasn't sure what to say to her. He knew now that he had nothing to worry about. Even though there was a moment he thought he detected something that made him just the slightest bit uncomfortable, but it didn't last long. He only wanted to protect her from the big bad wolf.

He knew Jay's type. Way too smooth and he had something about him that made lots of women flocked to him. He was used to getting what he wanted. Jay had Camille but, in her eyes and in her voice, Logan only sensed how much she wanted to get away from the wolf. Naturally, that was his job – to protect her.

Had Jay made it difficult for her to leave, Logan was pretty sure he would have knocked his ass out. He'd wanted to do that since he learned it was over a man that this beautiful woman nearly died.

Finally, she said something, "You do know that I'm done with him. I don't want him anymore."

"It would be okay if you still did. Wait, no it wouldn't. Not for you because he wasn't good for you, but I wouldn't judge you for wanting what you know. It's hard to break the cycle."

She didn't disagree. She crooked her finger for him to come closer. She whispered as if people at the park could hear them.

"The only cycle I want to break is the one where you've spent all afternoon not making love to me.

Smiling, he agreed. "Let's go handle that right now, forget the movies."

CHAPTER FIFTEEN

"DON'T DO IT!" Logan shouted loud enough to wake Camille up and then sat up in bed.

They made love all afternoon after he got off work. Barely taking time to eat anything but forcing down the strawberry banana smoothie she made for them both since he had been complaining of the gut he was getting from eating her food. Part of loving him meant she needed to look out for his health, so she planned to have healthier options for him when he was with her.

She quickly leaned over and turned on the lamp.

"Are you alright?"

"Yeah," Logan said still breathing hard. "I'm fine."

"Did you have a bad dream?"

"Yeah, but it was nothing," he said and sat up in bed. "Go back to sleep," he said and stood up moving towards the doorway of his room.

"Where are you going?"

"To get some water," Logan said in a clipped tone as he walked off.

He walked out of the room quickly and went in the kitchen. Logan leaned against the counter and tried to get control of his breathing. He pushed off the counter and began pacing back and forth.

I need to calm down, he said as he paced. *I can't let Camille see me like this.*

He opened the refrigerator and grabbed a bottle of water. As he drank it down, Logan thought that maybe he needed something stronger, but going back to bed smelling like liquor would just make her ask questions that he wasn't prepared to answer. Logan threw the empty water bottle in the trash and walked toward the bedroom, but he stopped before he got there.

He stopped and looked at his hands. They were shaking. Not bad, but they were shaking bad enough that it would be noticed. He had to get out of there, get some air and clear his head.

"Yeah, yeah, that's what I need. Take a ride to clear my head," he said, standing completely still and forced his hands to stop shaking before he went back in the bedroom. Logan went in the room and headed straight for the chair where he had laid his clothes when he took them off.

"Where are you going?" Cami said as Logan began dressing. "You're leaving?"

"For a little while. I just need to get some air," Logan said and tried to get dressed faster. The faster he dressed, the fewer questions he had to answer.

"What's wrong?"

"Nothing, Camille," he said and put on his sneakers. "Everything is fine."

"Then why do you need to get some air?"

Logan paused and thought of an answer because he didn't have one.

"I just do. You should leave though," Logan said quickly and left the bedroom and walked out of his apartment.

As soon as he closed the door, Logan leaned against the wall and exhaled. His heart was still beating fast and his hands were shaking. He had had these nightmares before, but this was the worst one yet. Usually, he was able to calm himself down rather quickly and after a while, he would be able to go back to sleep. But not tonight. He had to get out of that space more to avoid letting Camille see him like that. It was embarrassing. It made him feel weak and that was the last thing he wanted.

Logan unlocked the door to his *Volvo* and got in. He held his hands up in front of his face and made tight fists in an effort to will his hands to stop shaking. Once they complied with his will, Logan pressed the starter, rolled down all the windows and headed off. He jumped on the parkway and put his foot down.

Driving fast was kind of his thing and not with just the ambulance where his driving had saved many lives. Logan always felt the need for speed and as the speedometer inched toward ninety, his mind drifted to the place where he didn't want it to go.

It was just another night and he and Montane were sitting in the truck talking. They had just grabbed some dinner and had parked in one of their favorite people-watching spots to eat when the call came over the radio.

"I guess Stella and Carl are at it again," Montane said.

Stella McCarthy had been a frequent call of theirs. Either her neighbors or she would call 911 when her live-in boyfriend, Carl would beat her.

"I don't know why she stays with the bastard."

"Love makes people do strange things," he said as he pulled out with the sirens blasting.

"And how would you know anything about what love makes people do?" Shayna yelled over the sirens.

"I was in love once." Logan paused and took a haphazard look at Montane. "Once."

She laughed. "And that makes you the authority?"

"No, but I spent enough time talking to Noah and Amara to make me know enough to know that I don't need, nor do I want any of that in my life."

"Come on, Angel. There's got to be someone out there for you," Montane said.

"Yeah, well, if you see her, give her my number and tell her to give me a call. Until then, I'm riding solo," Logan said as they arrived at the address and went inside.

Montane knocked on the cracked opened door. "Life Rescue!" she shouted and walked in the apartment.

Usually, by the time they arrived, Carl would be gone. They would treat Stella's wounds and when the police arrived, she would tell them that she didn't want to press charges and they would all reset until the next time. So they entered Stella's apartment and saw Carl standing there and he had a gun. Logan immediately stepped in front of Montane.

"You called the police on me!" Carl shouted. It was clear he was inebriated and had a crazed look to him.

"I didn't call them!" Stella shouted back at him.

"Fuck you think you yelling at!" Carl shouted and pointed the gun at her.

"Whoa, whoa," Logan said with raised hands. "We're not the police. We just want to treat her wounds," he said, looking at the gash over her eye that he knew would need to be sutured.

"What ... you think I'm stupid!" Carl shouted and pointed the gun at Logan. "If you here, the cops is coming!" he yelled at the top of his lungs and Stella stepped in front of Logan which only set Carl off more.

"Fuck is you doing?" Carl asked and lowered the gun a little. "Picking him over me!" he shouted and pointed the gun at Stella. "You fucking bitch!"

"No! Wait!" Logan shouted just before Carl shot Stella in the head. The blood splatter sprayed Logan and Montane. Logan tried to stop what he saw happening in slow motion. Carl put the barrel of his gun in his mouth.

"Don't do it!" Logan yelled.

But it was too late. Carl pulled the trigger.

It was the cause of his nightmares. It was why he had been avoiding his mother. It was the reason that his stomach tightened when their number came up on his phone.

Now that his head was clearing, Logan realized where he was and he looked at the speedometer, he was doing ninety. He took his foot off the gas and watched the needle drift down. The car began to slow and Logan got off at the Edgewood/Swissvale exit. It was when he came to a stop at the light that he saw the blue and red lights come on.

"Shit!" he said aloud because he should have known better. Edgewood cops would pull you over at the drop of a dime. He pulled into the gas station, put the car in park and got his license and proof of insurance ready. Then he put his hands on the steering wheel.

"'Cause I don't want to be an accident," Logan said as the officer approached.

"License and proof of insurance, please," the officer said, and Logan handed it to him. "You were going pretty fast coming off the parkway. What's your hurry?"

"No hurry, officer."

"Have you been drinking tonight, Mr. Graham?" he asked and leaned in on the car.

"No, officer."

The officer stepped back and put his hand on his weapon. "Would you mind stepping out of the vehicle, sir?"

"No problem, sir."

Logan slowly opened the door and stepped out with both of his hands in plain sight. Admittedly as fearless as he'd always been, he was deathly afraid of being a victim of shoot first and ask questions later so often perpetuated by law enforcement. And he was afraid, even though many of his friends were cops. It didn't change the color of his skin.

The officer looked at Logan. "Angel?"

Logan leaned forward and squinted. "Daniels?"

"Yeah."

Daniels was Officer Ricky Daniels. He used to be Pittsburgh PD; they weren't friends, but they had worked several crime scenes together.

"Can I lower my hands?"

"Stop playing," Daniels said and took his hand off his gun. "How you been?"

"I'm okay."

"You *were* going pretty fast there."

"Yeah," Logan paused. "Just got a lot on my

mind. The job and all, you know, just trying to clear my head."

Since Logan said that he'd hadn't been drinking, Daniels stepped a little closer and took a breath.

"I know how that goes," he said, not feeling the need the give him a breathalyzer test. He knew that even if he failed, as a professional courtesy, he would make sure that Logan made it home rather than arrest him. "Sometimes, the things we see and the things we have to do on the job never leave us." Daniels shook his head as if really being affected by his own ghosts. "I can only imagine doing what you do. Sometimes you have to find a way to put it out of your mind."

Logan leaned against his car. "Sometimes I have nightmares about it," he said, speaking of it openly for the first time.

"That what got you out tonight?" Daniels asked and leaned on the car next to him.

Logan nodded his head. "Worse one yet."

"You okay now?"

"Yeah, I'm good."

"You headed home now, right?" If he expected Daniels to spend a great deal of time trying to get him to open up about his problems, he would have been wrong, but he didn't expect it. In fact, man to man, you didn't discuss these things. Being taught to deal in private about your problems and not to spend too much time dealing with them either, were the man's way. This is why he avoided telling anyone. It just wasn't what men did and certainly not what men did with their women.

"Right."

The officer stood up. "Good to see you, Angel."

"Don't call me that?"

"Huh?"

Logan paused. "Sometimes I don't feel like an angel."

"Why? You're the angel of mercy." Daniels chuckled. "You always get your people to the house alive," he said and tapped Logan's arm.

"Not all the time," Logan said sadly and exhaled. "I didn't get everybody there alive."

Daniels looked at Logan finally realizing that he needed to use some of his police skills. It wasn't all about fighting crime. In fact, a big part of being an officer was talking to people and helping them. Right now he needed to try to help Logan without over-stepping boundaries.

"Stella McCarthy?" he asked because he was there that night. He had seen the looks of anguish on Logan and Montane's faces as they sat there and watched the goings on at the horrific scene. Within a couple of weeks, he was transferred to a new police district and hadn't seen Logan again.

Logan nodded his head. "I couldn't save her."

Daniels was quiet for a moment as he thought about what he should say. "You know you can't save everybody," he said when nothing else came to him. "We want to. Shit, we're even expected to, but we can't; and yeah, it gets to me sometimes too."

"How do you deal with it?"

"I drink," Daniels said and laughed though he knew there were better ways to deal with things.

"Never been much of a drinker." And no matter what anyone said, he wouldn't become one.

Daniels pushed off the car. "Maybe you should start," he chuckled but then his voce turned serious. "Or go see a shrink."

"Not my style." Though he knew now he needed to talk to someone. Finally letting some of it out with Daniels felt good. He just wasn't ready to let it out with Camille and knew it would be awhile before he could if he ever could. He just knew that right now, he wasn't right for her. These nightmares were proof of that.

"Whatever you decide to do, slow it down," Daniels said and walked back to his car.

CHAPTER SIXTEEN

WHAT HE DIDN'T EXPECT when he came home from the gym was his woman playing Suzy Homemaker in the house. When he told her to leave, he knew it was a bit extreme and hurtful. It not only hurt her, but it hurt him deep in his soul to pull from her arms and tell her to be gone when he came home. He intended it to be hurtful in order to get her away from him.

Things between them were never supposed to go this far. That's what he told himself. They were just supposed to have a good time. His curiosity was really just about his superhero complex where he planned to fix her, get her back on her feet, and hopefully away from the man that helped to tear her down. That's what he told himself.

He also told himself that getting her away from Jay had nothing to do with his constant desire to have her. I mean, why would it be? From the time he met her, she was distracted with that dude. Camille had told Logan all about Jay, actually more than he thought he wanted to know. His role of friend before lover dictated that he at least listen to the situation that brought her to the brink of collapse so he listened but it pissed him off and after a while, he knew it wasn't about Jay being a terrible lover to Camille. It was about feeling something more than friendship for her. He should have seen that as a sign to bolt, but he didn't. He dug in. Wanted to know more about her. Wanted to spend more time with her. Wanted to see her smile. Wanted to be the one to make her smile. He then started to want everything with her and forgot how messed up she was and how utterly messed up he was. It started not to matter.

But it all did matter. It mattered that he couldn't have a restful sleep unless she was in his arms bringing her own brand of warmth that was white hot and perfect for him. And even that didn't always work, it didn't this night.

There were times he wanted to keep her with him but pinning her in that way was not fair to her.

Nor would it be healthy for him. What if she couldn't stand to be with him after a while.

He walked into the kitchen, and it smelled like something sweet. *She must be baking*, he thought.

She turned to the sound of his footsteps and tried to think of something witty to say about why she was still there when he told her to be gone.

"Why are you still here?" He asked.

"I knew you'd miss me if I was gone before you left. You needed to see me leave."

She was right, but that wasn't the point. He'd just have to get over missing her, but the pull of her light brown eyes threatened to make him forget why he needed to get rid of her.

"Camille, I told you already. You need to go."

"No, you talked, I listened, and I decided to stay. You love me. I know that Logan."

He said nothing. Denying it would be a lie but admitting to it right now would only make this harder. Why didn't women understand that just because it wasn't what you wanted, and it hurt like hell, didn't mean it didn't need to be done?

But then she sashayed over to him, placing her palm on his chest over his heart. His weak spot.

"I know you didn't mean what you said. I only stayed long enough to tell you that. I stayed long enough so you could see me walk out. So you knew that you made this decision to let me go – not me. That you know I love you and would want to fight for you but I'm not crazy enough to stay longer than you can tolerate and call the cops on me. I love you for who you are, Logan. Flaws, issues and all. I love you."

She kissed him softly. "But I will give you what you want," she said gently pulling away. "But you're going to miss me when I'm gone."

Logan watched Camille walk out of his apartment; watched her walk out of his life. He sat down and tried to convince himself that it was for the best. The best for both of them. It may not feel like it at the moment. He felt like someday, he would look back at this moment in his life and know that he made the right decision.

He stood up and went into the kitchen to grab a beer. *Maybe Daniels was right*, he thought as he grabbed the bottle out of the refrigerator. He made his way back and plopped down on the couch and thought about what he had just done. He remembered the pained look on Camille's face as she turned to leave. He did feel bad. Now he had caused her more pain and that was never his intention. She had already been through so much and all he had done by sending her away was add to that misery.

Logan imagined her driving home crying. A woman in love who had just been told by the man she loves to walk away. There was a part of him, *the weak part*, that wanted to tell Camille that he loved her and that he needed her. But that was selfish. He was messed up and she had been messed up and in ways still was. Both of them pretending to be fine, especially him. At least Camille was brave enough to own her pain, where he chose to hide from his.

"That's why she's better off without you," Logan said aloud and drained the bottle. "Maybe she can find peace now that I'm gone."

The following morning, Logan went to work and acted as if nothing life-changing had happened the night before. He needed to bury himself in his work that day. Problem was that he had worked side-by-side with Montane long enough for her to know that something wasn't quite right with him. However, each time Montane would inquire about it with, "You good?" Logan would answer, "Always all good," but she knew better.

So, they went about their day, saving lives. Their first call was a report of a stabbing. When they arrived, Logan and Montane were confronted with a man that had multiple gushing stab wounds and were able to get him to the hospital in time to possibly save his life.

They responded to a woman who was having a seizure. The patient had fallen and hit her head on an object, likely the end table, on the way to the ground, and the head trauma caused a seizure.

The afternoon came with them being dispatched to a cardiac call. When they arrived on the scene, they found the fifty-year-old man was suffering with chest pains and abdominal pains. As the day drew to a close, they were dispatched to a woman who was behaving erratically as if she were on drugs. But once Montane asked questions, they found that she was actually hyperglycemic.

"Just a case of high blood sugar," Montane said and once Logan nodded in agreement, she began the treatment.

At the end of the day, Logan had accomplished his objective; he had buried himself in his work, but it didn't work. Everything about his day reminded him of Camille. Each call he took brought him back to that night.

Pupils are reactive, blood pressure is stabilizing, skin is still clammy, cool to touch, he could hear

Montane saying, could see her administering the opioid reversal medicine.

Despite the fact that he had sent her away, he still needed to check on her, Logan still needed to know that his Camille was all right. He pulled over to the side of the road and put the car in park.

Logan reached in his pocket and took out his phone, but instead of making a call right away, he sat there holding it in his hand and staring at it debating if he should call and then decided it didn't matter if he should. He had to. Finally, he unlocked the phone, went to Camille's contact and was about to press talk, but he froze. He sat there with his finger poised over the talk button and then he shook his head.

"What would I even say to her?" he asked himself and dropped the phone in his lap. Logan was weak for Camille in all the best ways and he wanted to be with her. He felt peace when he was with her and he desperately needed to feel that peace, but that was selfish of him.

Camille doesn't need to get bogged down with my issues, but he needed to know that she was all right. The last time a man broke up with her, she almost killed herself, Logan thought as he picked up the phone, went back to Camille's contact info and sent her a text.

Are you all right?

Was all he typed and stared at the screen, waiting to see if she'd respond and wondering what he would do if she didn't respond. As he sat there, grim scenarios forced their way into his brain. All of the *what ifs?*

What if she went all alcohol and oxy again and this time, Amara wasn't there to call for help?

What if she didn't even make it home that night? What if she wrapped her car around a tree?

What if she needs you now?

He thought and felt the phone vibrating in his hand. He breathed a sigh of relief when he saw that his Camille had responded.

I'm fine.

That was her simple reply.

How are you?

I'm fucked up.

Logan deleted that reply and typed.

Good.

CHAPTER SEVENTEEN

SURPRISINGLY, Cami didn't cry as she left his apartment weeks before. For whatever reason, she was at peace when she left Logan. That could have been because she had always sensed this would happen. Things never lasted. People never stayed. She'd never had a relationship last. In fact, her relationship with Jay, notwithstanding their nasty breakup, was the most peaceful and long-standing relationship she had, if one could call adultery a relationship.

Despite her and Logan seeming to be perfect and starting off as friends then moving to lovers, she knew that he was still a mystery. There were things he didn't want to discuss with her and those things would eventually get the best of them.

Her life had been open like a book and not because she chose it that way, but because he came into the ugliest pages written in her life. He saw her nearly die. This was not a man she could hide from. But his dreams or nightmares, the ticking of his jaw when he thought she wasn't looking, and the tension he sometimes had in his shoulders told her he was carrying a heavy burden and he had yet to let her take even a bit of it from him.

Not that she planned to heal him. She just wanted to be to him what he had been to her. Balm. Love.

Her phone rang and she got excited thinking it might be him because though they hadn't spoken, he checked on her last week during a snow storm. It wasn't his number though. Cami didn't recognize the number.

"Hello."

"It's Althea, Jay's wife."

The next day, she went to Amara and her best friend shared some big news that had her quiet and reflective. Happy, yes, but quiet. That's because Amara again was living a beautiful life and Cami was still stuck. Of course, internally she was beyond her destructive behavior but the effects of it still lingered and she was beginning to lose hope that it would ever leave her.

"You seem sad," Amara pointed out. Her hand moved to her belly for the fifth time since Cami had found out her friend was pregnant.

"I am but it's not for the reason you think. I'm absolutely, positively excited about being an auntie."

Amara had finally spilled the news she'd been holding on to. She had intended to visit Cami after her sonogram where they saw the baby for the first time, but Camille showed up before she had the chance.

Amara smiled at her. Unable to contain the joy she had for her and Noah's future as parents. Even her fear that Cami's losses and her recent breakup with Mr. Man couldn't dim the overall excitement she was feeling. She was going to be a mother. This morning, Amara and Noah saw their baby for the first time. She was still marveling that she, the woman who ran more than once from Noah, was now his wife and soon to be mother of his child. To say she felt blessed seemed too small to describe this feeling.

"It's just that I've been thinking about all the things I did and didn't do. All the time I wasted on that man. The one you don't like to talk about. All the lies I told," Cami said.

"You've got to learn to let those things go, Cami. It's not who you are right now." Even if Cami knew that she had changed, the reality is, her relationship with Jay was one of a series of bad relationships. She had made bad decisions ... until Logan. And now they were done.

"I know that. I know he no longer has that hold over me but sometimes my pain does. You know?"

"I do. Remember all that running I did? Especially from Noah. Of course, I know. But look at what happened when I decided to stand still. Look at what was waiting for me? And I know some things are waiting for you also."

"I hear you." Cami paused before continuing.

"I got a call last night."

"From Jay?"

"No, his wife."

"What the hell did she want? She's done enough to try to ruin you. All for her philandering husband."

"Yeah. But I was foul, Amara. I was all up in his life. In almost every aspect of it and I'm sure she could feel me in it as much as I could feel her imposing on my life with him. Anyway, she called to ask me if he had been with me lately."

"The nerve!"

Cami just sat silently.

"You haven't, have you?" Amara asked gently, and with no judgement.

"No, not at all. I love Logan."

And she did. She really loved him. Her love for him made it clear that what she had felt for Jay was something else entirely. Not love, not quite lust, but brokenness seeking a place to fit. She hid in his brokenness and he in hers.

"I told her no, but he probably was with someone new. I expected her to get upset and start yelling, but she didn't. She asked me why I had to ruin her life. I wanted to be ugly towards her. Knowing all the shit she did to bring me down but instead, I decided to be truthful with her.

"I told her that she should never be worried about me. She should never be worried about any woman. That the one she needs to check is her husband. We aren't the competition. His need for something extra all the time should be her worry. I was one of many. Maybe I lasted longer than the others. Maybe I fit into his life a bit better. But eventually, he tired of me too."

"How did she take it?"

"Not sure but she had to take it because it's the truth."

After Camille left Amara's happy home, she thought about how she didn't mention her and Logan's break up. How she kept that to herself. Maybe it was because for once, she wanted to keep her problems to herself or maybe it was because she had resolved herself that their problems weren't really problems.

Relationships tend to ebb and flow. All that she'd been through over the past year told her to wait the tide out. If he was back with her, it was meant to be. If he didn't, well she didn't want to think that far yet.

CHAPTER EIGHTEEN

IT WAS early November and that day produced only more snow which was expected given the season and it being Pittsburgh. Not only was it unexpected, but it was heavy and that meant accidents. Logan and Montane had responded to a vehicle extrication and positioned their vehicles to consider routes of travel to the hospital and protection from traffic but allowing rescue and fire suppression equipment adequate space.

As they approached the hot zone, Logan saw that the vehicle was a black two thousand fifteen *Chevy Impala*. His heart began to beat faster. Camille drove a black two thousand fifteen *Chevy Impala*, so he walked a little faster. As he was trained to do, he immediately began a detailed evaluation of ongoing vehicle stabilization, safe patient access, disentanglement of the vehicle from the patient and extrication of the patient from the vehicle. In doing so, Logan was satisfied that it wasn't Camille.

Logan may have satisfied himself that it wasn't her in the car, but as he continued to size-up the scene, looking for evidence that the driver was alert and reactive, his mind was on his woman. But that was nothing new. But remembering Camille saying that she wasn't the best driver in the snow, Logan pulled his phone from his pocket and sent a text.

Are you all right?

While he continued to survey the scene and assess the situation in case his assistance was needed by the fire squad, Logan held the phone in his hand and it vibrated.

I'm fine.

Logan quickly and excitedly tapped out his reply.

Please drive carefully. It's getting bad out here.

Thank you for thinking about me but there's no need to worry. I am in for the duration of the storm.

Glad to hear it.

How are you?
Good.

As Montane shook her head, Logan put his phone back in his pocket and got back to work evaluating the scene's safety measures. Although it had been a month since he'd last seen or spoken to her, Camille was always on his mind. She was the reason for everything that he was doing. The time that Logan had spent away from her made him realize how happy he had been with her. If he were ever to experience that happiness again, he needed to get his mind right before he could be with Camille or any other woman; not that there was any other woman for him.

For most of his life, Logan had always been the type of person that was perfectly content to drift through it. He did the things that he wanted to do and did whatever it took to do it. For years, he'd worked jobs until they no longer challenged and amused him, and then it was time to move on and do something else. It wasn't until he thought that being an EMT might be challenging that he found something that he wanted to not only stick to, but to become the very best at it.

That was the way that he had come to see Camille. For most of his life, his relationship with women had gone the same way. They were cool until they no longer challenged and amused him, and then it was time to move on.

Camille was different, and he'd spent a lot of time thinking about exactly why that was.

To begin with, what he briefly shared with her came from a different place than almost all of his relationships with women. Even though Logan had always thought that she was beautiful and sexy. He'd tried to get with her at Noah and Amara's wedding. What he felt for her now and what they shared didn't come from a place of lust.

It began with deep felt compassion and concern for somebody he knew. That compassionate concern spawned a friendship and that turned into love.

Love.

Logan thought and realized that if what he felt for Camille was love, and he knew it was the day he told her to leave, then he'd never been in love before.

It was too bad that he was so screwed up during the short time that she loved him like no other ever had. Had he been in a better frame of mind, it might have been beautiful. Therefore, Camille was the catalyst of his quest to get his mind right. It may be too late for him and Camille, but he had to move beyond the space he was when he sent her away for his own salvation.

It began a week ago when he opened up to Montane about it. When he did, she laughed because the after effects of that night affected her too and she'd been keeping it from him and trying to cope on her own and in her own way.

"How's that working for you?" Logan asked his partner and she laughed.

"It's not," Montane paused. "Tequila and random sex with multiple partners haven't been an effective treatment."

Even though they had experienced the same traumatic event, in all the time since, Logan and Montane had never talked about it. Never talked about how they felt beyond each asking the other, *are you all right?* immediately after it happened. The following day, they did their jobs as if it was just another day and two people didn't die before their eyes the night before.

"We deal with blood and death every day," Montane began. "And we deal with it. So, yeah, I tried to play it like it was just another Saturday night at Stella's."

"Yeah, only this time he finally did what we've

all been saying that he was going to do and killed her."

It was the talk at the scene. Just about all the first responders that were there that night had responded to a desperate call from Stella. Each time, Carl would be gone when they arrived, Stella wouldn't want to press charges, and all would leave with the same thought in mind.

"One day he's going to kill her."

And he did. He shot her in the head.

"At least the bastard was nice enough to blow his brains out and save the tax payers the cost of a trial and locking his sorry ass up for life," Logan and Montane had heard more than one cop say that night.

That at least opened an environment between them where they could talk about that night and how they felt. Since neither had any interest at all in seeking some type of counselling, even though they both agreed they probably should, they tried to heal each other with friendship.

Logan had to admit that talking things through with Montane was helpful with the day-to-day, but it had done little for his reoccurring nightmares.

No! Wait!

Logan would see Carl shoot Stella in the head,

blood would splatter on him and Montane, Carl would put the barrel of his gun in his mouth, pull the trigger and Logan still woke up screaming, *don't do it!*

There was another positive thing that had happened over the last six weeks. The somewhat fractured relationship between mother and son had healed itself. It was easy. Since his problems were the real problem and her only real problem was that he was avoiding her, showing up for dinner when he was able and going back to calling to talk on a regular basis ended that. Surprisingly, that worked out better than he thought it would.

Maybe it was his growing ease with his issues and he attributed that to he and Montane's therapy sessions with each other, or it was just that his mother stopped asking what was wrong with him. But in either case, it was working. It was Sunday and he was hungry.

"Who's winning, Dad?" he shouted when he let himself in and heard the game on.

"Your father's not here," Andrea said, wiping her hands on her apron as she came out of the kitchen. "He ran to the store."

"During the game?" Logan said and hugged his mother.

"That's what I said."

"He must have been out of cigars or something."

"You know your father. He rushed out of here cussin' but glad the *Steelers* are the late game."

Mother and son stood in the living room and watched the next play which was a run for no gain.

"How are you doing?" she said and turned to go back in the kitchen. And since it wasn't the *Steelers* playing, he followed her in.

"Doing great, Ma."

"That's good," Andrea said as she opened the oven. "You look good," she said, inspecting him. He just smiled.

"What are we having?" he asked, leaning in for a peek and seeing mac and cheese, sweet potato pie and rolls baking before she closed the oven.

"All that you saw pork ribs and turnips."

"Where's Doreen?" Logan asked and sat down at the table.

"That new man she's dating surprised her with a trip to the Nemacolin's Resort.

"The ski resort?"

"Uh huh."

"Doreen doesn't know how to ski."

Andrea sat down at the table. "That's what I told her."

"What she say?"

"Told me that was the point," she said and they both laughed. Logan relaxed and looked forward to a quiet afternoon with his parents because Doreen would not be there to annoy him for her own amusement.

Andrea looked at the smile on Logan's face thinking that he looked happier than he had in a while.

"Whatever happened to that nice woman you said you were spending time with?"

"We're not seeing each other anymore."

"What did you do to run her off?"

"What makes you think that I did something?"

Andrea tipped her head to one side.

"You're a man. Men always find a way to mess things up." She patted his hand. "You just can't help yourselves."

"Well, you're right. We were happy together and I found a way to mess things up," Logan paused. "I loved her and I sent her away." Logan laughed at his own stupidity and looked at his mother. "For her own good," he laughed. "Stupid, right?"

"I can't rightfully say since I have no idea what you're talking about."

Logan laughed but it was an uncomfortable one. "I guess you don't, do you?"

"But I'd like to," Andrea said and squeezed his hand.

"Her name is Camille Douglas," Logan began and told his mother their story. "The first time I saw her was at the dress rehearsal for Noah's wedding," he began and told her everything. "After that, I started to go over there to check on her. You know, just to make sure she was all right."

"And since you were kind of sweet on her anyway," Andrea said as Mark came in the kitchen.

"Sweet on who?" he asked and leaned in to kiss his wife on the cheek. "What y'all talking about?"

Logan and Andrea looked at each other.

"You might as well start from the beginning," she said and she was glad that Doreen wasn't there to continuously interrupt with annoying remarks.

"Her name is Camille Douglas, Dad," Logan began again and told his father their story. "And we were pretty happy, I guess, until I told her that it was over."

"Why did you end it?" Andrea asked, and Logan reminded them of the night Carl killed Stella and then took his own life. How could they forget, it was on the news for days and their son was involved?

"I have nightmares about that night," Logan said and told them about the nightmares for the first time. The effect it had on him and how he allowed it to ruin his relationship with Camille.

"Because I couldn't save her," Logan said and his chin dropped to his chest.

"What makes you so arrogant to believe that you had anything to do with whether those people made it to the hospital alive or not?" Andrea asked, shaking her head. Logan had no answer.

Mark shook his head. "I thought we raised you better than that, boy."

"That responsibility falls to the All Mighty and Him alone. Just because some people on your job call you an angel, don't make you one."

She stood up and went to the stove to heat up the vegetables.

"It's not your fault that man killed that woman. You were there to help. You don't have the power of life and death," she said.

"You're just the driver," Mark said.

"A driver *in service* to The Lord, but the responsibility is and always will be His, and His alone," Andrea said, taking the food out of the oven. "Now, go make yourself useful and set the table."

"Yes, Ma."

The Graham family enjoyed a nice quiet dinner together and then they watched their *Steelers* beat the snot out of *Green Bay* before he went home. Logan drove home thinking again of his stupidity. His mother had simply and plainly put it all into prospective for him and he wondered why he had spent all those months harboring in his pain instead of seeking his mother's wisdom.

He walked in his apartment and went straight to the refrigerator to get a beer. He sat down on the couch, turned on the Sunday night game and put his feet up knowing that he had made a major breakthrough. He hoped it would put an end to his nightmares and then he could move on.

"Maybe it's too late for me and Camille," Logan said aloud and then he thought about Amara's baby shower and his intention not to attend for fear of ruining it for everybody.

"Or maybe it isn't."

CHAPTER NINETEEN

POSITIVE.

Those were the results of the pregnancy test she looked at on her bathroom sink.

She was pregnant and by a man she no longer spoke to every day. A man she missed more, and not less, each day. A man she loved more than she could have imagined. He fathered the child growing inside of her and right now, she didn't know how to tell him.

At first, she had no idea what was wrong with her. Her healthy appetite and metabolism dictated she eat lots of meals throughout the day but for the past week or so, she had been feeling queasy. She had no desire to cook or bake, let alone eat. And then she had a revelation while watching a movie where the heroine realizes she had missed two periods and what that had to mean. The parallel was alarming.

She herself had missed a period. Now that she thought about it and would be approaching another in a couple of weeks, but she didn't have her familiar ovulation pangs that signaled that. She immediately shut off *Netflix* and headed to the drug store to purchase a multi-test box and rushed home. Her heart pounded the entire time and the queasiness only increased as she went through the process of reading the instructions. She squatted, urinated and then waited for the result. She tried to busy herself as she waited but nothing worked. She found that she needn't had waited the three minutes the instructions outlined because it was almost immediate. The second faint line that said her discomfort was for a reason.

She had been here before and it wasn't pretty. She had been here twice. The first time, the baby was beaten out of her; the second, she allowed to be taken from her and one might think she'd learned from her mistakes and use birth control but the hormones had always given her horrible side effects like irritability, spotting and constant bloat so she had stopped taking the pill while with Jay. And if she were honest, she had let down her guard with him, foolishly believing that if she had become pregnant, she could handle raising a child without him being there all the time. Not realizing he would not even want even a part time responsibility to a child with her. So after everything she went through, birth control was not on her mind and still wasn't after she started to be with Logan and they used condoms most of the time but there were a few times they were caught up in each other and went with the flow. How could she be foolish again after all she'd been through?

So while other women might feel excited, even with the prospect of doing it alone, she felt guilt. Remorse and sadness. Did she even deserve the honor of carrying life when she seemed to not take care of the ones given to her before?

But almost immediately, she remembered something Logan had told her.

You are worthy of all good things, Camille. No matter what you've done or had happened, you are here. You are now ready to receive love and you will also give it. Accept it; accept joy.

It seemed like such odd advice coming from a man, and not a woman. For a man, he had one of the deepest souls she had ever experienced and that was saying a lot given her best friend was Amara, the deepest girl on earth.

Logan had provided her with shelter, a place where she could lick her wounds, rest, heal, grow, smile, laugh, love and trust again. He had done it without asking for a thing in return, though she knew if he had, she might not have been able. That was the moment it all made sense. He was gone so that he wouldn't break her. Again. He feared she'd not be able to handle whatever had him jumpy and restless.

But she was healed now. Well mostly. She still felt some guilt over her affair with Jay and she didn't know whether she'd ever get over that, but she'd have to try. She was about to bring another life into the world.

Her stomach grumbled as a reminder that she hadn't eaten anything but toast and mint tea. She grabbed her purse and coat, bundled up and left out to go to her favorite Vietnamese restaurant where she could sip on some pho while she came up with a plan to support herself and her child.

After parking in a lot and making her way down Walnut, she started to pass a baby consignment shop and was pulled in. The *Ultimate Creation* was high-end so she knew she wouldn't be able to afford anything in there even if it was second hand. This store was located in an affluent section of town so the items likely cost more than a few months of her teacher's salary. She went in anyway and looked around. Her mind on the possibilities of her future. She tried to think of a way to at least get Amara a gift for the gender reveal party that was happening in two weeks.

"Camille," a familiar voice said. She turned to find Ms. Dundy or Ms. Carol, as she was known to Cami.

"Hi, Ms. Carol!" She hurried to give Amara's mom a hug and enjoyed the embrace. Her mother always gave the best hugs and from spending time over Amara's house over the years, she had gotten plenty. Ms. Carol had tried to be a surrogate mom to Cami but admittedly, Cami was in a bad place after her mom died and avoided allowing anyone to counsel her or to love her. So she would try to wiggle out of being around Ms. Carol for long periods of time because she didn't want to have any talks that would remind her that she didn't have a mother. She had always felt that was on her. She was to blame.

As part of this time of reflection and healing, she began to realize that nothing could have prevented things from happening as they did. Some horrible person killed her mom, not her. And though she could have been a better daughter then, she was a better person now. The person her mother would have wanted her to be.

"Hi, baby. I thought that was you when I came into the store, but I got so caught up in all the pretty things that I was distracted for a moment. You in here shopping for the baby?" She asked.

Confused for a moment she just stared. How could she know about the baby when she just found out herself?

Unknowing, Ms. Carol went on to say, "My first grandchild will probably put me in the poorhouse if I get anything from here, so I understand if you were just looking."

Recovering, she laughed while fingering the price tag on a onesie hanging on a rack, "Yeah, I'm just looking. Definitely not buying."

Smiling, they stood side-by-side for a moment. Both looking at the baby clothes and then Ms. Carol grabbed a canary yellow onesie that said, "YaYa's baby."

"This is perfect. My grandchildren will be calling me YaYa. I made that decision as soon as those two got married."

"I love the name, Ms. Carol. Let me walk you to the register." Even though Cami had no intention on buying, she didn't want to leave Amara's mother just yet. It was like she needed something first and didn't know what it was.

Her stomach chose that moment to rumble again and it must have been loud enough for Ms. Carol to hear it.

"Baby, you want something to eat? There's a place down the street here that serves Vietnamese. I was going to grab something from there."

"I was just on my way there," Cami admitted.

"Well join me, baby. And I don't want to hear you are taking it to go. No, we will sit and talk."

She had no choice but to relent and hope that she didn't reveal she was pregnant. She wanted Logan to be the first to know.

After ordering a bowl of vegetable pho for her and Carol ordered the marinated honey chicken, they started to chat.

"So what's been going on with you, Cami? You doing better?"

"Yes, Ms. Carol. I'm much better. Every day I feel more like myself or my new self." In addition to journaling and talking to her dad more, she started seeing a therapist. Just someone to talk through the big things and to avoid going back to that ugly place she ended up before. She would need to be able to cope with change, good and bad.

Ms. Carol smiled. Amara must have gotten that smile from her. It told Cami she knew more than what she had chosen to reveal.

"That's good to hear. Amara didn't spill the beans, but I knew enough."

Their food arrived, and they began to eat.

"The important thing is that you heal," she continued.

"Yeah, some days are easier than others. I've been feeling guilt."

"From what, if you don't mind me asking?" She knew Cami had an affair with someone and it turned ugly.

"For being with a married man. For it turning ugly."

"Oh," was all Ms. Carol could say. After a moment, she observed Cami and decided to open up though she suspected Cami wasn't in the dark about how Amara came to be.

Carol's relationship with Amara's father may have begun years before he married and they were supposedly done. He had moved on, went in the Navy, got married and had children when they started their affair. That led to Amara and some deeply ugly experiences that Carol hated to even think of. That was until she realized Amara couldn't learn how to move forward in her own life until she dealt with the pain of her parents' history.

But if Carol were going to be all the way transparent, she'd admit to Cami that she and Russell, Amara's father, were not done. They had a new beginning. Recently, they cruised together and were openly dating. Just not broadcasting it. Carol's mother was supportive but, of course, her sister and brother had mean things to say and she was just happy none of it hit Amara, who had enough to deal with.

"Well baby, I have my own story like yours."

Over the next fifteen minutes, Carol shared her affair with a married man, the outcome, and how she moved on.

"After a while, I realized that I was wrong, but I made no greater mistake than many women who fall in love with the wrong man. I didn't break a vow. He did. I just broke my own heart. I would have to repair it by loving myself again. Making loving decisions, being loving, speaking with kindness, and just being happy.

"Amara helped with that. Seeing her happy

became important to me and I knew I had to be a part of that experience."

Cami listened intently and felt like there was no better person to have ran into that day. Ms. Carol understood and with that, she knew she had to let all her guilt go. It wasn't good for her anymore. It wasn't a part of loving herself.

"I understand, Ms. Carol."

"You can always come to me about anything, baby. I'll be here."

"Thank you so much," she nearly whispered.

Teary-eyed, she went back to her soup.

"You don't want anything else to eat?" Ms. Carol asked when she pushed her bowl away from her.

"No ma'am. That hit the spot."

Ms. Carol eyed her suspiciously before smiling that Amara-like smile again.

"Maybe I should have bought more baby items."

Essentially implying she knew that Cami was pregnant, even though Cami never revealed it.

CHAPTER TWENTY

IT WAS two weeks later and Cami sat amongst a host of friends to celebrate and find out the gender of Amara and Noah's baby. Gender reveal parties were all the rage and these two wanted to be trendy when it came to their first born.

Cami and Carol cooked the food and decorated the house. Noah, Logan and Mr. Douglas did all the running around for supplies, namely drinks and whatever else they distracted themselves with to avoid being in the women's way. Russell was there to provide the music though everyone could see his eyes remained on Carol who seemed to be switching her hips a lot more, to Amara's horror.

Maya and Roman Newsome were accountants and as a side business, were consulting for Noah's firm. He invited them because they were both parents and Maya seemed to love everything about Amara, whom she deemed serious but happy looking in the picture that sat on his desk. Stacy and Quentin Edwards were invited by default because they were visiting Maya and Roman. Maya being a bit shy asked Stacy, really forced Stacy, to attend after first making sure it would be okay.

Amara, who was short on friends unless Cami brought them, immediately said yes. Then there was Joseph and Savanah who were positively glowing and though they still weren't married, Mr. and Mrs. Farrington said it wouldn't be long because, "You too are like rabbits. Soon enough one of those *we'll be right back* excuses will turn into a baby." Everyone laughed and even under her deep brown skin, Savanah blushed.

The other Farrington brothers, their wives and children were there and a few other coworkers and friends.

The gender reveal part happened so quickly everyone wondered why there was a party. The mistake was made when Joseph and Noah's back and forth teasing went too far and Noah said, "At least my son won't be scared of cats."

The room grew silent and everyone watched

Amara's face get tight and she ran from the room crying.

Noah went after her and after a few moments where they all silently chuckled, afraid the hormonal Amara would hear, they returned. Amara seemingly happy.

"Boy, that smile of yours could charm the skin of a snake," Russell said.

Everyone laughed, including Amara who couldn't argue. Noah had always been able to bring out the best in her in any situation.

But despite all this activity, both Logan and Camille stayed on opposite sides of the room. They didn't despise each other but because they wanted each other, their separation would have made it awkward to admit to it.

After a while, none of the commotion, festivities and their own avoidance of each other could keep them from finally speaking to each other. It seemed everyone was looking on as Logan approached Camille and asked her if she would step into the kitchen with him.

A few moments later, they were ensconced in the galley-style kitchen, where Logan had slid the door closed so they could have much-needed privacy.

After a few short tense moments of the two of them just staring at each other, he finally said, "You look good, Camille. Damn good."

She wondered if what he saw was the glow every book she had read said a woman got when carrying. Amara's, who was now seventeen weeks, was just now feeling better. Whereas Cami, now eight weeks, started to feel better last week and had taken upon herself to scarf down everything, though all of it was healthy food. She knew that Logan would flip if she ate horribly. That is, whenever she finally told him, which looked to be right about now.

"Thank you. You look good too." And he did. His skin always looked like a light glowed from within his bronzed brown skin and she wondered if he were really an angel. A fallen angel who helped save her with his love.

"We avoided each other long enough, don't you think?" He asked her.

She nodded in response and then said, "Yeah, I think we've avoided each other long enough. How are you, Logan?'

"Missing you," he responded without a breath.

"I've missed you too," she said breathlessly. This was going easier than she thought. She had hoped they could just pick up where they left off.

"Then come here," he commanded.

She moved closer to him an allowed him to pull her into his strong embrace, where he held her close to his heart. She nuzzled there, breathing in the scent of him. The scent of his fresh skin. She truly missed him.

"We shouldn't be apart like that anymore," he said into her thick hair.

"I agree," she said into his chest. "I didn't like it very much. Neither did the baby."

"Who's baby? Amara and Noah's?"

"No, ours," she said simply.

Camille pushed away so fast she nearly fell forward but his hands held her up. She braved it and looked up at him to see if he was upset.

"We're having a baby? How?"

"Well, I guess it was all those times you just couldn't pull out if a gun had been put to your head," she joked weakly.

Still shocked, he observed her. She was worried he was upset. He wasn't. He was very shocked and happy, to be honest. Camille was right. There was no stopping with her. She was perfectly made. Nothing but warmth, softness, tightness, wetness, and deepness. He had to have it all when he was with her or die trying. Well, he guessed all that trying produced life and he was beyond excited. Scared too, but he knew he and Camille could handle it all.

"I'm happy Camille. I know you will be a great mother and with me by your side. Our baby will live a good life."

Teary-eyed, she just moved into his arms again and he held her.

"Just don't do something stupid and ask me to marry you," she said.

"Why not?"

"I don't want you to marry me out of obligation. I want to marry you because you love me and want to be with me."

"I do love you and want to be with you."

She pulled away and looked up into his brown eyes again.

"Camille, marry me? I'm ready to make it right. You are the woman for me and I'm done hiding from that."

She thought about it. Thought about if they were rushing. She surely hadn't imagined coming away from this party with a man, let alone a proposal, but here he was and it felt right. Nothing else in her life fit as right as this. Everything seemed to be coming together for her.

The school board heard her appeal and she got

her job back on the condition that she have no contact with Jay Taylor, whose wife had already removed Ali from her school in the middle of the school year. She had found out the news that Ms. Douglas would be returning.

She was sad about not having Ali in her class, but also knew the drama that would come from her remaining there would be disruptive. Jay hadn't reached out to her after she informed him, through email, that his wife called and that she would appreciate it if any suspicious behavior he displayed had nothing to do with her.

Now having her job back, she had some security. So last week, she went back and she bought their baby a rattle from *The Ultimate Creation* and was able to get Amara something too. And now this.

In the end, she knew they weren't in a rush at all. In fact, both of them had spent their life rushing to get away from anything that remotely looked and felt authentically like it might be a beautiful thing. As if they didn't deserve love, but here they were. Two beings in need of love and gave it to each other. Love was always required for them to move forward and they did.

"Yes, Logan. Yes, I will marry you," she said.

Also by Aja

I Am Yours

One Night

Good Old Soul

Love's Required

Love Taps

She's Got Soul

Deep In My Soul

Tease

The Swan

Unexpected

Be With Me

The Pursuit

About the Author

Aja is the writer of sensually erotic and passionate women's fiction. Her stories allow readers to experience realistic, inspiring, and soulful interactions and intense passion while overcoming life's challenges. She is inspired by soulful music and sensual art to craft her stories.

www.ajathewriter.com

ABOUT AJA

Aja is the writer of sensually erotic and passionate women's fiction. Her stories allow readers to experience realistic, inspiring, and soulful interactions and intense passion while overcoming life's challenges. She is inspired by soulful music and sensual art to craft her stories.

www.ajathewriter.com

Made in the USA
Las Vegas, NV
03 November 2021